ROSES ARE RED SO IS YOUR BLOOD

RICK WOOD

BLOOD SPLATTER PRESS

ABOUT THE AUTHOR

Rick Wood is a British writer born in Cheltenham.

His love for writing came at an early age, as did his battle with mental health. After defeating his demons, he grew up and became a stand-up comedian, then a drama and English teacher, before giving it all up to become a full-time author.

He now lives in Cheltenham, where he divides his time between watching horror, reading horror, and writing horror.

ALSO BY RICK WOOD

The Sensitives

The Sensitives

My Exorcism Killed Me

Close to Death

Demon's Daughter

Questions for the Devil

Repent

The Resurgence

Until the End

Blood Splatter Books

Psycho B*tches

Shutter House

This Book is Full of Bodies

Home Invasion

Cia Rose

After the Devil Has Won
After the End Has Begun
After the Living Have Lost
After the Dead Have Decayed

The Edward King Series

I Have the Sight
Descendant of Hell
An Exorcist Possessed
Blood of Hope
The World Ends Tonight

Anthologies

Twelve Days of Christmas Horror
Twelve Days of Christmas Horror Volume 2
Roses Are Red So Is Your Blood

Standalones

When Liberty Dies
The Death Club

Sean Mallon

The Art of Murder
Redemption of the Hopeless

Chronicles of the Infected

Zombie Attack
Zombie Defence
Zombie World

Non-Fiction

How to Write an Awesome Novel
The Writer's Room

Rick also publishes thrillers under the pseudonym Ed Grace...

Jay Sullivan

Assassin Down

Kill Them Quickly

The Bars That Hold Me

A Deadly Weapon

© Copyright Rick Wood 2020

Blood Splatter Press

Cover Design by bloodsplatterpress.com

No part of this book may be reproduced without express permission of the author.

Roses come first
Violets for mains
Then for dessert
I'll eat your BRAINS

WHY WON'T YOU TALK TO ME?

WHY WON'T YOU TALK TO ME?

WHY WON'T YOU TALK TO ME, SALLY?

This weekend hasn't been quite the weekend we expected it to be, has it?

I mean, I've done what I can. I have spent the last three days trying, helping, complimenting you and talking through our problems and you still just sit there.

Propped up at the table.

Your dinner untouched.

So cold in your silence.

There is nothing I can do anymore, Sally, there really isn't. I have taken you to this cabin, I have made you dinner, I even spoke to your mother when she called and you refused to pick up the phone.

I told her you were fine. I told her *we* were fine.

We are fine, aren't we, Sally?

"Please," I say, and I hate the begging in my voice. It sounds so desperate, so lost, so hopeless. I used to pity men like me, really, I did. I used to look at them with their apathetic wives and think, gosh, that will never be me.

Now look at us.

Your expression hasn't changed. Your eyes still stare at the floor, your head lulled, looking anywhere but at me.

"Look at me, Sally," I tell you. "Look at me."

You don't.

I see no movement. No giving in. No surrender.

"Why won't you just—"

My fist clenches and I feel my anger grow, and I tell myself, no, stop it. My anger drove us to this. My anger made us what we are now.

I need to control it.

But you don't reply, knowing it will incense me, like you are provoking me; like you want an excuse to tell everyone I'm a nasty, violent man.

Well I won't give in. It won't work. I won't do it.

You've seen me mad before, but not now.

I am not like I was before. I am going to stay grounded. Stay level-headed. Think clearly.

You stink, Sally. You really do. It's like you purposefully didn't shower so I won't touch you. Like you thought it would put me off. Anything so we're not naked together. Anything so sex is not an option.

We made love last night, Sally. You were there. Don't you remember?

Except it wasn't love. You barely moved. You just lay there and took it. Let me finish while you stare at the door.

You always stare at the door; you always have. Since day one, every moment we spent together you would be checking where the door is.

This weekend could have been so much better.

I turn away. Pick up the phone. Dial 999. Tell them where I am. Where you are.

They will think I kidnapped you, but I didn't. You came here willingly.

Three days of bliss, of us being *us* again. That's what you promised.

Three days of open talking and good times.

It was meant to make us stronger, but it's killed us both.

We have a few minutes, Sally. We have a few minutes until the police get here. What should we do, Sally? What should we do?

Sally?

Sally!

Fuck's sake, Sally, come on.

Don't do this.

"Please," I say, and I find myself on my knees, taking your hand in mine.

Your hand is stiff. You don't place your fingers between mine, but you don't move away either.

You used to be so full of life, so vibrant. Young and energetic. We used to have sex all day and talk all night. We used to enjoy being naked together. Hell, we used to enjoy each other's company in whatever state we were in.

Have I driven that out of you?

You still won't look at me.

"I didn't mean it," I insist. "I didn't, honestly, really, it just happened, I don't, I…"

I trail off.

What can I say?

Sometimes there is nothing to say.

I hear the sirens.

I bow my head. Close my eyes. How I'd love to just sit here and listen to your breathing, but I can't do that anymore. You won't let me.

"Why won't you let me, Sally?"

Why won't you?

The sirens are so loud now. They are outside. I see the flashing lights reflecting on the fridge door.

They will take me away now, Sally. They will. But we will always be together. Remember that.

We will always be together.

Always.

They kick the door open. They didn't need to as it was already unlocked. They bind my hands behind my back and read me my rights and I know, Sally, I know that I will never see you again.

* * *

Detective Inspector Jackson Lyle stands in the kitchen.

His colleagues take the man away, and for a moment, it is just him and the suspect's wife. Sally Benfield.

Then the Scenes of Crime Officers enter and setup.

Lyle waits outside for them to finish, and for the pathologist to arrive. His name is Daniel Stephens. He's a good friend.

Once Daniel has finished, he approaches Lyle and offers him a cigarette. He takes it. They stay in comfortable silence until Lyle finally asks the question he dreads to ask.

"How long?" he says. "How long has she been like that?"

Daniel sighs.

"Three days," he says, wondering if they'd managed to find the rest of her body yet.

Roses are red

That is for damn sure

These are your flowers

And this is my CHAINSAW

ME AND MY STALKER

1
NOAH

I first saw you on Tinder and, honestly, you didn't stand out.

I mean, it's tough to stand out in an app that shows you face after face after bikini after face.

You had a bio almost identical to many other boring women on the app.

Suniya, 23

Heartbroken. Not interested in fuckboys. Like painting.

Suniya not my real name.

Well no, of course Suniya is not your real name. Your Caucasian skin gives that away. But that's not the worst part.

To demonstrate what I mean, let's break down what you have written, Not-Suniya.

Heartbroken: yes, who isn't?

Sorry, but this really frustrates me.

Everyone gets their heartbroken.

I mean, EVERYONE.

What makes your pain so unique, Not-Suniya?

Nothing.

You have been through a breakup that hurt, just like everyone else. You probably cried just like everyone else, and you probably cursed the man who dared cause your boring pain, just like every other man or woman who has been in your position.

There is nothing special about the way you're feeling. Don't think it's appealing to hear you moan about it.

Next: *Not interested in fuckboys.*

You're on Tinder.

What the hell do you think you will find?

I say that, fully aware that I am searching on Tinder for a long-term venture — but I am also aware that I have to veto and bypass the majority of wenches who fill my phone screen. Occasionally, I may come across one worthy of my time, only to message them and find they have no concept of how a conversation works.

For example, one such conversation I recently had went like this:

Me: How are you?
Her: I'm good thanks.
Me: What do you do?
Her: I'm a nurse.
Me: Do you enjoy it?
Her: Yep.

Generally, when someone asks a question, one asks a question in return, and doesn't just give blank answers. It is impossible to hold a conversation with someone who does not engage in said conversation.

And, finally, the way you finish your dating profile bio: *Like painting.*

If I ignore the awful syntax – the omission of the word *I* to begin the sentence – then I can appreciate actually hearing something about you that is of worth. Honestly, Not-Suniya, I would have led with this.

Your profile, being so typical of the attention-seeking miscreants I constantly swipe left over, inspires a feeling of wrath inside my belly.

I decide to learn more about you, if only to spite your attempt at secrecy. You seem to believe a fake name will make you difficult to find, so I endeavour to prove you wrong.

I screenshot your picture.

Search for it on Google.

(Few people seem to realise that, as well as words, you can also search an image on Google – making it easy to find a person with just their face.)

Your Facebook account appears top of the search results.

And there you are.

Easy as that.

Your name is Stella Celeste.

Now that is a lovely name. Why not use it, Stella-Not-Suniya?

You have long, blond hair, but I can see from both your freckles and your past photos that you are actually ginger, and I'm saddened that you haven't kept your natural hair colour. Maybe you grew tired of being teased at school, but you should have ignored those bullies as there's something so sexy about a fiery redhead. After looking through even more of your photos, however, I can see that you change your hair colour as often as you change your boyfriends. I don't know whether you're indecisive, or have another breakdown every time you get dumped that prompts another attempt at reinventing yourself. There are only so many times, however, that you can reinvent yourself until you have to come to terms with being that same insecure mess you were the first time you announced a change of personality.

I've counted at least eight pictures of you giving the peace sign. You don't do this because you believe in peace, necessarily; not that you're against such a concept as peace, but that isn't your reason. You do it because all the American celebrities in the videos you watch on YouTube do this and you desire, so keenly, to be one of them. As if mimicking those with fame will somehow validate you. As if being like these people you worship means you have a chance of being one of them someday. I presume that you wouldn't care what you are famous for, even if it's something that makes everybody hate you, so long as everyone recognises you.

In fact, there is a recent Tweet by you that suggests as such:

The only way to succeed is to make people hate you. That way they remember you. — Josef Von Sternberg #ainthatthetruth #quoteablestella #hatemebitches #likeIcare

There is a reply to your Tweet asking who Josef Von Sternberg is and you haven't replied, which sums you up, Stella. You quote a man and you don't even know who he is.

You wear big necklaces. Not metal or silver necklaces, but necklaces made of string with some kind of big circle on the end of them. Occasionally its yin and yang, sometimes the peace symbol. As if you know what they mean.

You're just trying to masquerade as a hippy. In truth, you stand for nothing, do not go on marches, and do not believe in happiness for all. But you smoked a bit of marijuana once and dressed to fit in with a friend you once had, and you believe this image gives you depth.

If anything, it stops you from standing out. It makes you fade into the background. It makes you less special. And that, I imagine, is the one thing you fear above all else: not being special.

Your skirts are sometimes long and flowy, but most of the time you wear tiny shorts or tiny skirts.

Oh, and what's this? A bikini picture.

You have a gorgeous body, but that's not why you posted it, is it? Not because of pride. It's because of a need to feel wanted. A need to grow your self-esteem. This image has been placed here deliberately. Men from your Facebook have commented below, saying things like *wow sexy lady* and *fit* and, instead of being disgusted, you like their comments and even thank them for it.

I bet you know that most men on your Facebook have wanked over this picture, Stella — and I bet you like it. When a van passes and honks at you, unlike most women who would feel unsafe or disgusted — you frown on the outside and jump on the inside.

You want to be wanted.

Being desired is the only thing that gives you a fleeting burst of confidence.

You write about literature on your profile — classic literature, not new. You think this gives you depth. Or maybe this is the only honest thing about you I've seen, Stella.

You like Dickens. You have a status on your wall you wrote last Christmas:

Great Expectations and A Christmas Carol. Two books to read every year.

Maybe you read A Christmas Carol every year. Maybe it's for pleasure. Or maybe your father read it when you were a child, and so you read it every year in desperation of re-finding that feeling you had when he read it to you; that Christmas tingle.

But you're a grown-up now, Stella. You reject adulthood, but that doesn't change reality. You still work in the same café you worked in as a teenager. You don't have a mortgage or a career or a relationship that you want. Because that would be something an adult would do.

You hate being an adult.

But don't we all, Stella?

We don't become adults because we wish to.

And that's why you are so desperate for a man to hold you. Not so you can feel love, but so you can feel protected like you felt as a child, as fleeting as the feeling was.

But you can't be protected.

You have to face the world.

Maybe I should be the one to help.

I am already obsessed with you, Stella.

I am already infatuated.

And I think it's time that we meet.

2
STELLA

It's always like a contest with guys I meet online as to who can bring the dick pics out first.

Tinder has the fortunate lack of ability to send pictures, but there's always the point in the exchange when whatever half-handsome, barely witty imbecile I have matched with asks for my number, and the conversation gravitates over to WhatsApp or iMessage.

After a few messages like *how are you* and *what are you up to tonight* and *you look pretty in your picture,* when it seems like it's going well, I look at my phone and they have sent an image.

WhatsApp warns me that this image is potentially offensive. Silly WhatsApp, I say, thinking the lovely picture — that I assumed is of himself or his dog or his dinner — is offensive. I click open.

And there it is.

Like a demented slug, or the leaning stem of broccoli, or the sad spine of a flower.

I mean, I am sure you are proud of your appendage

(though very few times can I see why), but I did not ask or invite this image to be sent to me.

So why does it keep being sent to me?

One thing I can say, however, is at least I can learn before I meet these men that they are pricks. Can you imagine if I went to the trouble of putting on a face of make-up, buying a new dress, and giving up an evening of my life to discover that this narcissist only wants a quick shag.

I mean, honestly, I put *no fuckboys* on my profile to eliminate men like this. Didn't seem to work!

I dream of finding someone honest. Someone real. Someone who will laugh with me about the hypocrisy of politicians flaunting their right-wing agenda; who will share intellectual discussions about great works of literature with me; who can make my body shake as much as he makes my lips smile.

Not some pale pervert with a receding hairline and aggressive pride about their inadequate penis.

Maybe Tinder just isn't the right place for that.

I do what I do any time life's quandaries pull me away from potential happiness — I take to social media to vent.

Apparently my potential Romeo comes with unprecedented dick pics. Who knew? #really #firstworldproblems #itsnotthatbig

I slide my phone into my pocket and put on my apron, ignoring the poster on the door of the break room warning that all phones must be left in lockers while working.

I fluff my hair, straighten my blouse, and pull up my skirt.

I don't need a mirror to tell me I could look better. I have four hours of a shift hanging off me, and I can't wait for a bath and a book.

Need me some alone time with the right kind of Dickens #bath-night #isworknearllydoneyet

I leave the staff room and walk into the café. A guy works on a laptop, two women talk, and a man walks in, making brief eye contact with me before sitting down.

This man's hair is messy, but deliberately so, and I like it. His eyes are wide and his body is toned and his skin is clear.

He's a good-looking guy; then again, aren't they all?

3
NOAH

SHE LOOKS AT ME AS I ENTER.

Our eye contact is brief, but purposeful. I make sure it happens.

She said she was working here in one of her many public social media posts. She seems intent on broadcasting all of her movements for everyone to see.

That will have to stop, Stella.

I'm sorry, but I'm not having you interrupt every minute we spend together to post another tweet or snap or Insta or status about what we're doing. The world doesn't need to know we're eating or are on the bus or are fucking; that can be for us.

Is anything just for you, Stella? Or is it for the entire world to see?

You are at work. On shift. Serving coffee. Yet you look effortlessly impeccable. Your hair is straight, mascara subtly applied, your skirt and blouse impractical. You care more about appearance than comfort, don't you? But it's important to you, isn't it? That even when you are at your worst, you present your best.

I've seen your social media, Stella — you are all about image. You need people to believe you are perfect.

Or maybe it's just in case the man of your dreams walks through the door, and you dress every day like you're waiting for me.

Well, here I am, Stella.

I have arrived.

And I am ready.

I take a seat by the window and watch the world go by. I want you to think I'm deep, the kind of deep that will match your shallow interpretation of deepness. You want the kind of man who can argue about the composition of Dicken's language, as if it matters, as if you're not just arguing about pretentious nonsense.

But I'd do it for you, Stella.

I'd do anything for you.

I take out a notepad, so you think I'm writing something.

And I take out Great Expectations.

No one writes and reads a book at the same time, Stella. It's ridiculous. You don't do both; you do one or the other. But you will not care. You're just going to appreciate the appearance I create.

You're walking over to me. You're about to take my order. So I smile.

Not a teethy smile or a beaming grin.

No, I give you *the smile.*

The kind of smile that says *hey you.*

Not the kind of smile that peers at you lecherously, or appears awkwardly dorkish. This is the kind of smile that makes you flutter, that makes you blush, that makes you look at me and fall in love.

You meet my eyes and I see that stare, and it's an attraction stare; it lingers just that bit longer. I look back into those green eyes and think about all those songs that go on about blue eyes — but those songs are wrong. It's green eyes that are the most captivating; like a go sign to your soul.

I'm ready to go there, Stella.

"Hey, sweety," you say, as if it's endearing, but it's what your aunt calls your uncle and it's not sexy; there are so many better things for you to call me.

You're better than that, Stella.

I order a latte and, as you walk away, your eyes linger on me. When you return, you reach your arm out, and place my coffee in front of me. You could have done this around the other side of the table, but you want to reach your arm across me. You aren't wearing short sleeves but your sleeves are rolled up, meaning I have to see those freckles on your arm and smell your skin before its wafted away.

I know it's just an arm, but it's so much more. Just like the few buttons on your blouse you leave open, meaning that, when you lean in, you can't help but tease me with a few bits of lace on your bra.

Do you show this to everyone, Stella?

Of course not — you know what you're doing.

"Need anything else?" she asks.

I smile and shake my head, and that's when I take it out.

A battered and dog-eared copy of Great Expectations.

"Are you a Dickens fan?" she asks, slightly startled.

Good-looking and a reader of literature? I might just be too good to be true...

"Not all of his stuff," I answer. "More just this novel. Oh, and A Christmas Carol. Two books to read every year, don't you think?"

Her lip hangs open and she stutters over a few syllables. My, she's astonished.

"Yes," she finally says. "Yes, I do."

Wow, you are speechless. It's as if I took the words right out of your mouth.

I didn't; I took them right out of your Facebook feed.

4
STELLA

He's saying these words like he sprung them from my thoughts. The familiarity of his observation is both surprising and endearing.

I already know I'll lose all confidence and won't be able to ask him out. For all I know, he's just humouring me.

How do I keep falling in love so easily?

"Two books to read every year, don't you think?"

He looks at me with a cheeky half smile, like he knows something. Like he knows me because he knows himself; he sees a look of recognition in the twinkle of my eyes and God, I thought moments like this only happen in Disney movies.

"Yes, yes I do."

I say four useless words because my lips produce nothing profound.

I wish I could say something that sums up the discovery that the only good-looking guy who shares my specific belief in literature is sitting here before me — but all I can do is stutter and think about how I still need to fetch the guy on the adjacent table his muffin.

"Thank you, Stella," he says, ending the conversation, and

just like that, it's over.

But I don't want it to be over.

So I say something not only the opposite of flirtatious, but almost accusatory.

"How do you know my name?"

What is wrong with me?

It's a question with no conviction and no real meaning – a question that shows how I am always on the defensive. Why is that?

"Your name tag," he says, nodding to the pin badge over my left breast.

He looks at my breast, but it's just to read my name.

And now I'm disappointed I'm not being harassed?

He smiles at me.

I'm still there.

I'm still looking at him.

At this point, really, I'm just hovering.

I am so awkward.

So I go and get that guy his muffin.

I make more people their coffees, get more cakes and take more money, and the entire time I just keep looking at him, knowing I'm doing so in an entirely creepy stalker like way, but unable to help it.

He doesn't look up once.

He doesn't glance at me. He must feel me watching, but he doesn't meet my gaze, doesn't turn his head. He just keeps his face in his book, reading about Pip and Mrs Havisham and Estella, and how I wish I could be *his* Estella.

Now that was creepy. I'm attaching us to the love-struck characters of a romantic masterpiece.

We've barely said two words to each other, but I am already imagining our wedding day and the brilliant speech he'd give. I can see us on our deathbed, holding hands as we talk about the wonderful life we've lived together.

Truth is, he will finish that chapter just as he's now finished his coffee, he will put it in his bag, and he will leave.

And then what?

I will obsess over someone else. Anyone else.

God, why do I do this?

All it takes is a smile and one trait we have in common and suddenly I've planned out our old age deaths.

He puts a bookmark in his book.

Places it in his bag.

Stands.

Puts the bag over his shoulder.

He doesn't look at me. Doesn't even divert his gaze in my direction. Just readies himself for an imminent departure.

I'm about to let him walk out. About to watch another potential suitor walk out of my life because I didn't have the guts to say something to him.

I tell myself it's fine.

He wasn't that great, anyway.

It probably wouldn't have worked.

Sure, the first few months would be great. We'd get excited, text each other all the time, say we miss each other, have copious amounts of sex, fall asleep naked…

But after six months to a year, it would grow stale, and it would die. It would wilt like my unattended plants.

Love is not a cactus. It can't endure dry spells. It is a rose chosen from the supermarket, already separated from the earth, something beautiful that you can prolong with a bit of water in a vase but will ultimately need throwing out two weeks later.

He goes to leave.

But he doesn't; he walks toward me, and he stands there, barely looking in my direction but standing in front of me, nonetheless.

This is my chance.

Come on, Stella.

But I say nothing.

I always say nothing.

"Have you got a bit of paper?" he asks.

At first, I am stumped, no idea what he's said or how to react.

"I, er, yeah," I say, then feed a bit of receipt out, pull it off, and give it to him.

"Thanks," he says as he takes it. "Could I borrow a pen?"

I am equally flummoxed. It's as if he's just asked me to explain black holes and quantum physics.

After an excruciating wait, I pull a pen out of my pocket and hand it to him.

"Cheers," he says, not looking at me.

He writes something on the bit of receipt paper and hands it to me. I take it, staring at him, and he winks at me — he goddamn winks, and I think I may have just gotten a little wet — and he leaves.

I look down at what he's written.

It says his name: *Noah.*

And beneath that is a phone number.

I almost jump to the sky, almost fist bump the air; then reality brings me down.

For all I know, this is some practical joke. He saw me staring, and he decided he'd write the number of some sex line or his grandma or something, thinking it would be hilarious.

Things like this only happen in movies.

Oh, for god's sake, stop it.

It's *his* phone number.

It's *Noah's* phone number.

The only question now is — how long do I leave it?

Scrap that, the question is — how long *can* I leave it?

5
NOAH

I HAVE TO PUT THE PROVERBIAL BALL IN HER FIGURATIVE court.

I have to make it her choice. Her decision.

By giving her my phone number, it is now up to her.

But she will not use it straight away, will she?

Hell, she may not even use it today.

Because she has to play games. She will want to make me squirm, waiting for that call; she will want me to wonder whether she will even use that number — then, just at the very moment I think it will not happen, I will so gratefully clutch the phone as that unrecognised number prompts the ring tone.

But I'm not stressing, Stella. Really, I'm not.

Because I know you'll call.

I take a bit of time away from her. I don't want to get obsessed, do I?

I return home to my bedsit and put the radio on. I have a television, but I never use it. I just want some background noise, and Radio 4 is playing some documentary program about an old jazz player, and that will do me just fine.

I go into my bathroom.

Except, it's not just a bathroom, you see.

It's also my dark room. I have blackened the windows, and pieces of string hang from one wall to the other, with photographs developing on each one.

Photography is my passion. I loved it before it became the fad of every white woman in her twenties with a digital SLR and a black and white filter. It seems like anyone trying to appear deep cites photography as one of their hobbies — but it's not really a hobby for them, is it? Everyone has a decent camera on their phone nowadays, and it's easy to just take a picture, and it's easy to have decent composition, and it's not something that women in their twenties with a fancy camera can really stand out in anymore.

Because *good* is something anyone can be.

But I am beyond *good*.

I am *magnificent*.

I don't just take photos. I capture beauty. I encapsulate metaphors. I steal moments of lives.

It is not about the composition, or about the filter, or about the angle.

It is about the subject.

It is about what you are capturing, and how you feel about it.

There is a photograph developing of an old lady that lives in the doorway to a shut-down, bordered up tattoo parlour in town. She sells Big Issue magazines and lives in her sleeping bag. People often walk by and offer her their umbrella when it's raining, or a drink when it's hot.

But no one ever offers her a permanent solution to her misery.

I took a photograph of her while she was sleeping, and her closed eyes are just fading into view.

The issue with this image, however, is that I do not give a

shit about this woman. I don't know her backstory. For all I know, she deserves her position in life. Or, she may not, and may be a victim of abuse or drugs.

Either way, the photograph has no fire behind it; no affection toward what I'm capturing.

Now, this photograph beside it — that photograph is pure artistry.

It is an image I immortalised whilst I was in the pub the other day. I found myself draining my pint of beer quickly and tearing up the corners of the beer mat as I did. I wasn't even aware of myself doing this.

They say ripping your beer mat is a sign of sexual frustration, but honestly, I wasn't that aroused.

So what made me tear up the side of this beer mat?

I was not feeling anxious. I was not feeling perplexed or confused or any kind of conflicting emotion.

So why did I do it?

That's why I took a picture of that beer mat, with its logo still in view, the corner ripped and frayed. That beer mat meant something; the way I tore it up had a purpose, but I do not know what it is. It is an unexplained phenomenon to me. A perplexity I can't fathom.

And that is why I preserved it in the permanence of a sheet of photo paper.

I leave a few more photographs to develop as I eat. One of a water fountain, one of a pencil case, and one of a dead person's face. I have cheese on toast for dinner. Two. With tomato sauce. I squirt the tomato sauce into a smiley face, just like my mother used to.

I didn't have a fucked-up childhood, by the way. Nothing went wrong. My childhood was so good it was practically made up.

Although, I did always begrudge my mother for not being a stronger woman. She allowed my father to push her around and tell her what to do and put her down when she voiced an opinion he didn't like.

I finish my tea, and I leave the house.

Finding out where Stella lives is easy. She moved into her flat six months ago and posted a picture of her and her friend, a pretty black girl with bushy hair, outside their new flat. I can see flat number sixty on the door behind them, and she tagged her location, which tells me which street to look for.

It takes twenty minutes to walk there and I can see into her bedroom window. She wears a vest and pants. The curtains are open. It's as if she wants me to see.

Her mobile phone is in her hand.

She paces back and forth.

Oh, Stella, stop playing games.

I know you want to call me.

6
STELLA

I GO TO THE GYM AFTER WORK. I REALLY DON'T WANT TO, BUT I feel like my size eight dress is getting a little tight, and I dread the thought I might be putting on weight. I may even skip tea tonight, who knows... In the meantime, I spend the next forty minutes doing circuits. I take a picture of myself in the mirror as I do it. I look a little sweaty, so I apply a Juno filter on Instagram that instantly improves my appearance, and I post it with the caption:

Good bodies take hard work #gymlife #norestforme #carbs-bedamned

Forty minutes pass quickly, and that's good. If I'd spent that forty minutes doing nothing, I'd have been too tempted to call him already. Instead, I waited a further forty minutes.

When I return to my flat, Lancelot strokes my leg and I feed her.

Lancelot is my cat, FYI.

Freya isn't here. Even though we moved into this flat together, I barely see her. She practically lives at her boyfriend's house. If her half of the rent wasn't paid, then some months I wouldn't even know if she was alive.

I take off my gym leggings. I stand there, waiting to put my pyjamas on, holding my phone. I wasn't aware of picking it up, nor did I realise I had also picked up Noah's number, but here it is.

How long has it been?

Four, five hours?

Surely it's too soon?

I don't know, how soon is too soon…

I google it. I type in:

How long should you wait to call a guy?

The first result is an article on *the three-day rule.*

Three days?

Please, I struggled with three hours…

I feel like he'd have lost interest by then. Would have forgotten me. Would have walked into another coffee shop and met another woman and given her his phone number, and that woman would have rung that same evening, and they would have begun a blossoming relationship where I'm barely an afterthought.

No, I can't wait three days. Surely. He'd have moved on by then.

Another article is entitled *It's Okay to Reach Out to a Guy in Less Than Three Days.*

Ah! Now that is comforting.

The next result is a survey on Match.com that says a third of men thought less than three days was appropriate.

A third?

This is really not going well.

I put the phone down.

Shall I just call him?

I will call him.

No, I can't call him.

I put my pyjamas on. They are warm and cosy in a way that a man can't be. I snuggle into them and enjoy them, but still wish I had someone to cuddle.

I bet Noah gives nice cuddles.

I bet he gives excellent head too. He looked like he had a good mouth. I bet he's generous. Close to his mum, but not too close, not in a creepy way. Close in the way that means he's learnt to be respectful toward women.

Maybe his dad left, and he had to look out for his mum.

I wonder if he would look out for me, then remind myself that I am an empowered woman and don't need to be taken care of, even if it would be nice.

I bet he drives a cheap car, but he's not annoyed about it. In fact, he's proud; he worked for that car, however crappy it is, and he doesn't need an enormous car to compensate for anything.

God, what is wrong with me?

I haven't even phoned him, and I've already invented his backstory.

It's as if, instead of talking to him, I'm better off talking to the imaginary version of him.

I wonder if he could even live up to the image I have in my mind.

I wonder if anyone could.

Fuck it, I think.

I pull out the number.
Pull out the phone.
Close my eyes, take a deep breath.
Give myself permission to do this.
And I call.

7

NOAH

I FEEL IT VIBRATE IN MY POCKET AND I WAIT, JUST BECAUSE I know it will infuriate you.

I see your number; I see the screen light up, and I can't see you anymore from where you sit, but I can tell you are hating every agonising ring.

Eventually, I place the phone to my ear, answer it, and say nothing. I sigh, as if I'm groggy, as if I've been sleeping, as if it's a bad time.

"Hi?" I groan.

"Hi, is that Noah?"

Pause.

"Who is this?"

"I, erm, it's — it's Stella. From the café."

I take a few seconds to remember.

"Stella! Hey. How you doing?"

"Is this a bad time?"

"No, no, it's a perfect time. In fact — just hang on one minute, yeah?"

"Okay."

I put the phone by my side and pick something out of my

teeth. At least, I go to pick something. There's nothing there. Don't know why it was uncomfortable.

I return the phone to my ear.

"Sorry, I'm back."

"Are you sure this isn't a bad time?"

"No, really, it's fine. I wasn't sure if you'd call. I thought it was corny, like something out of an old-fashioned romance movie. I felt like I should have done it in black and white or something."

Her favourite movie, as stated in her Facebook bio, is Casablanca, and I can practically hear her stifling a squeal. Aren't I just so bloody perfect for you, Stella?

"Yeah, I, er… I thought it was pretty cute, actually."

You'll hate yourself for saying that. You don't want to seem too keen, but I reckon you've already pictured our wedding day.

Don't worry, Stella.

I've pictured it too.

I'd pictured far before we ever met.

"And here I was cursing myself for being such a dork."

"There's nothing wrong with a bit of dorkiness. We could all be so dorky…"

Get to the point, Stella. I don't want to have to be the one who asks you out.

"So why did you give me your number?" she asks.

Why the fuck do you think?

"I don't know. I thought I saw you looking at me. I thought you were… I don't know. I feel I've already said too much."

"No. No, I like it."

Of course you do. Not because it's charming and endearing, but because it makes you feel like you're wanted.

If I didn't like you so much, Stella, I would resent you.

"So," she says, dreamily, and I can see you now, walking

around your flat, fiddling with the silk of a dress left over a chair, running your fingers over the knobs of the oven dials, rimming the top of your wine glass. "Are you going to ask me out?"

Oh, very direct, Stella. I am surprised. You are desperate to ask me out but cannot fathom the words, so you coerce me into doing it. Either it is very sexy and flirtatious, or mildly infuriating — but doesn't that just sum you up?

"I was considering it."

"Well..."

"I made the first move already. I dropped my number off. Shouldn't it be you asking me out?"

And this piece of flirtation will really test you, won't it? Do you disgrace yourself by being the one to ask me out, or do you continue to coerce? You know it should really be you; you are a feminist after all, and should be empowered enough to ask out the man.

But your ego won't take that, will it? Like so many women, you are a feminist when and where it suits you. Women like you are the reason that feminism fails, you spoilt brat.

I apologise, Stella.

That was harsh.

You're insecure, I know.

I'll let you off.

I'll break you out of the agony.

"How about a drink?" I ask. "Are you free Friday?"

You wonder if two days away is too keen, but then again, I'm the one who suggested it — so agreeing to it won't be keen, or so you tell yourself.

"I'll meet you at seven," she says.

"Perfect. Shall we pick a place, or..."

"Surprise me."

You pretend that making me pick somewhere to go is

elusive and sexy. Really, it's because you're so indecisive you can't function, but do not want to reveal such a flaw.

"I'll text you a place."

"I will look forward to receiving it."

"Good night, Stella, lady from the coffee shop."

"Good night, Noah, man who came to the coffee shop."

I hang up and, right on cue, you emerge into the window, hugging a teddy that was probably bought for you by an ex – your daddy would hardly get you a teddy, would he? I doubt he cared enough.

You remove your pyjamas and run yourself a bath. You feel like treating yourself.

Very reckless, Stella.

Any perverted voyeur could see your body through the window should they look hard enough.

And anyone could have just taken a picture on their phone.

And anyone could use this picture for less than honourable actions, Stella.

Best start getting in the mood for Friday night.

8
STELLA

I DECIDE THAT I DESERVE A BIT OF PAMPERING TONIGHT.

I made the call. I did the talking. I took a leap of faith.

The bath calls me, as does my Kindle, as does a nice dose of *me* time.

He likes Dickens.

He knows how to flirt.

He knows how to smile.

Gosh, did he know how to smile. And to wink.

I can see him now, winking, smiling that cheeky grin, and looking up at me, and saying, "Do you want more?"

And I want more.

And I tell him I want more.

And god, how I want more…

9
NOAH

We agreed to meet on Friday, and we agreed that on the Wednesday.

I am immensely excited, so when I wake on Thursday, I am most perturbed to find myself with a day to spare. It would be best if I was kept busy but, unfortunately, I fear the time may pass slowly.

I glance at my phone screen. I have an email confirming a wedding booking.

I love photography. It is my life's joy, my all-consuming passion. However, it is a sad truth that, when someone has a creative art as their job, they have to use that creativity in situations they don't particularly wish to, to make a living. A writer may have to write a genre they don't enjoy so they can make money from a more popular genre. A pianist may have to play in the background of a party where people speak louder to be heard over the melodic hum of their unappreciated tune. A comedian may have to perform to a bunch of inebriated, uncaring, rowdy men on a stag party in the backroom of a pub so they can earn the right to perform to more pleasant audiences.

Similarly, I have no choice but to provide photography skills at weddings to get by. As well as christenings. Children's parties. Family photoshoots.

People are not interesting subjects for my camera lens. People are dull. The same. Full of monotony.

I like to capture moments of interest, perfecting my art by encapsulating actions that would otherwise go unnoticed by humans too self-indulged to notice them.

No one notices the way the wind pushes leaves into an entrancing form of symbiotic dance. It's like the leaves curtsey to each other, then crash back and forth like they were in a mosh pit.

No one notices the life of a bogie transferred from a child's finger to the base of a public bench. I would watch that bench all day, capturing the people who eat lunch, kiss, frolic, smoke cigarettes, and meet friends on that bench, none of them noticing the remnant of an infant's vulgarity just beside their thigh.

And no one notices the beauty of water. The way it reshapes and directs its own path. Everyone is too busy thanking the god they were taught to believe in rather than appreciating the beauty of a world moulded by nature, not by fate.

But, when a couple stand at the front of a church full of relatives and friends who discreetly slag them off, that is the moment they want to capture; and it's so dull that I have to remind myself how much I need the money. I walk around talking photos, hearing the snide comments about the wedding; unappreciative criticism of a day tediously planned and financed to hell.

Human nature is to be cynical and nasty. I'm not interested in noticing that.

The worst part is that I need a Facebook page to attract clients, and I cannot have a Facebook page without having a

Facebook account; so I've reluctantly set one up with extreme privacy settings and the function where no one can add me without having mutual friends.

But I have to have this account, as I need clients.

Without clients, I can't eat, or finance the bedsit where I spend my evenings masturbating. Honestly, I've spent so much time watching porn that the sight of a naked woman in real life doesn't even hold my erection anymore.

That is why I don't want to lose the potential of you, Stella. I imagine your female form will encapsulate and enthral me like no other woman can achieve.

And I don't believe you're like everyone else.

You aren't bitchy at weddings.

You appreciate the beauty of water fountains.

You aren't boring.

At least, I hope you aren't, Stella.

You show the image of your ideal self to the world. You decorate your social media with the life you wish to present. And, if that was you, I would not be interested, I really would not.

But I'm interested because I'm fascinated by what's behind it. The woman you keep away from the public flaunting you do so liberally.

Speaking of which, I am yet to check your social media today.

Let's find up what you're up to, shall we?

It's barely eleven in the morning yet, and already there are three status updates.

7.02 a.m. I would like to have a strong word with whoever invented this time in the morning. I don't need a job that much, do I? #first-worldproblems #boomornings

7.14 a.m. I'm up now and do you know what? It's not that bad. Life is for living. And when something exciting happens, you can't help but wake up with a smile on your face. Let's go, world! #coulditbe-happening #luckygirl #happygirl #pleasedtobealive

8.12 a.m. On the bus #thewheelsgoroundandround

I'm not much of a morning person too, Stella, so you needn't worry. But I can't help wondering if it is my introduction to your life that has introduced the spring in your step that is so clear in your second status. Could it be that I have brought some happiness to your constant moaning?

I love and I hate this part of a relationship.

I love the excitement, the untapped potential, the possibilities.

I hate that it will probably end.

Right now, I am a dream to you. I am a guy who smiled at you and charmed you and left you his number. Once you get to know me, what will I be then?

I've had this before.

Most women are after the unattainable. I seem interesting, and I seem like a good idea, but as soon as you have me, as soon as you feel like I'm not going to leave, that security you are after removes the magic and *boom* it ends, just like that.

I am determined not to allow us to be like that, Stella.

I am, however, slightly put out by your last status update. We needn't be told that you are on the bus. There's already something mildly annoying about someone who shares every thought and feeling on social media, but there is something even more annoying about someone who shares their everyday actions.

Do we really need to know that?

I mean, do we? Really?

I decide to spend today getting to know you a little better. I would have gone to your flat to watch you, but now I know you are on the way to work. So that is where I will go, Stella.

Not that you'd have any idea that I'm there.

10

STELLA

IT'S JUST ONE OF THOSE DAYS.

It seems like any great high is followed by a great low.

I spent the whole of last evening with an enormous smile. I sat in the bath, smiling; cooked some pasta, smiling; went to sleep, smiling.

And it was as if, when I awoke, the universe was looking at me, thinking, *ah, well, we can't let this last...*

And, like any bad day, it is caused by an isolated action committed by a single person. It's so sad, isn't it, that one fool's inconsiderate nastiness can bring an entire life to its knees?

As soon as the bastard in question walks into the cafe, it's as if he thinks the chime of the bell above the door is there just for him, just to mark his entrance, announce his presence. He saunters in with the stride of a cage fighter entering the arena. I only notice him because his lecherous eyes are on me with such an intent stare that I can feel them latching on, awaiting my curiosity.

I ask him what he would like, and he doesn't even reply. Just stares at me.

What the hell am I meant to do now?

I know he's trying to make me uncomfortable. A stronger woman would tell him she will not tolerate it. I just stare helplessly, wishing I knew what to do.

"Well," he finally says, looking at the nametag covering my breast, as if its placement is just an excuse. "Stella," he continues, and I'm surprised this oaf can read, "what have you got for me?"

What have I got for you?

Such an alluring question. If I was to call him on it and say that I can tell there is obvious sexual innuendo, that he is harassing me, he would just be able to use the excuse they all use — *What are you on about? I was talking about in the café, like cakes and stuff. Jeez, women like you are so uptight...*

It's what people good at harassment do. They groom you and make you think it's your fault. They make you feel disgusting and grotesque and abhorrent in a way that they could easily claim I have misinterpreted.

What, you think CCTV will pick up the way he's staring at me right now? You think my manager, a tired man in his forties who once aspired to so much more, will care? You think there is anything I can do about it?

No. This is where society fails. When a young woman is completely and utterly alone. When a young woman just has to accept the degrading nature of such men's advances.

And anyone who tells you I have a choice is lying.

Honestly, sometimes it's tough to keep the belief that a nice guy exists at all.

"Well," I say, forcing an air of professionalism, "we have a wide selection of cakes today, we have different types of coffees, and we have a selection of paninis and sandwiches."

"Is that right?" he says, then watches me again, just saying nothing.

In his mind, I'm naked.

In his mind, I'm on my knees with my mouth wide open begging for his slimy cock.

In his mind, I am disgusting.

"If you can't decide, sir, then I can always serve someone else while you—"

He leans over the counter. Honestly, there's no one else to serve, so it's an empty suggestion, anyway.

"I like it when you call me sir," he says.

I've been presenting a smile.

I've been presenting the front I know I should present.

But now I really, really feel alone.

"Please stop," I say, though my voice comes out small and tiny.

"Stop what?"

"This. Just choose what you want and be done with it."

"Just choose what I want, eh?"

I bow my head. Close my eyes.

That isn't what I meant.

Why is no one helping me? Why is no one coming to my aid? There are at least ten or twelve people in this café at the moment; why can't any of them see what is going on?

Everyday sexism doesn't bother passers-by. It isn't until harassment leads to rape or suicide that people half-heartedly question what they could have done.

"Please, just choose something, or I will have to ask you to leave."

I hate myself for the lack of conviction in my voice, for the empty threat. Like I could do anything to make him leave. Like my manager wouldn't just apologise to him and serve him instead.

"As you wish," he says. "How are the bagels? Are they warm?"

"Just tell me what you want."

"Well..."

"What food. Or drink. Just... please."

His grin seems to fill his face.

"I'll have an Americano. Milk. No sugar. Bagel. Cream cheese. Ham. And anything else you might offer?"

I ignore the question.

I get him his damn bagel.

I pour him his damn coffee.

But it's not over.

He doesn't take them to go.

He sits on the table closest to me and stares. As he eats, chewing with his mouth wide open, he watches me, barely blinking.

I want to scream at him, *why are you doing this?*

Why me?

What is it that made you get up this morning and decide you would make a young woman feel like shit?

Why this person, in this café, in this town, at this moment?

Were you bored? Opportunistic?

Was this pre-determined or did you just...

I don't know.

I hate it.

I hate how a man I don't know makes me feel like this.

I hate how no one cares.

And I hate how there is nothing I can do.

11
NOAH

I WATCH YOU.

And I understand you now, Stella.

I understand why you are this insecure. Why you have to parade the intricacies of your monotony over the internet. Why you are a person who needs the approval of strangers so you can feel validated.

Because the world hates you.

Because this is what it does to you.

It makes me feel sorry for you.

It makes me want to protect you.

And, most of all, it makes me want to save you.

I want to save you, Stella. I want to take you away from this life and show you that a man can treat you right. That you can find someone who will not stare at you for the sake of ruining your day, for finding an opportunity when you are isolated in a job you can't lose and using it to make you feel…

I can't imagine how you feel.

But I can still stop it.

Come with me, Stella. We'll run away to a place where we don't need mundane jobs. We'll get rid of my bedsit and we'll get rid of your dead-end career and we'll find new lives; lives where we can be what we want to be.

You leave work that day and you don't let the world see it. You will not stop in the street and risk a stranger asking why you are upset. You wait until you are at the bus stop. When it's dark. And you are alone. Almost alone, that is; there is an old lady with her wheeling bag, but you stand far enough away from her that you can be discreet.

And that's when you do it.

You bury your head in your hands. You cry silently so this old lady doesn't notice; she wouldn't notice anyway, but you won't risk it. You cover your face and your body convulses as you sob.

It doesn't last long.

Eventually, you pull your hands away and wipe them across the base of your eyes and feel your cheeks.

Your hands rest on your legs and they scrunch up your skirt; you pull it into fists, gathering tufts of material, crumpling it — and I bet that's where you cut yourself, isn't it? I bet your thighs are covered in scars beneath that skirt. You'll probably stop me from going down on you so I don't see them, Stella. But I see them.

Because I see you.

The bus arrives, and you leave, and it's time for you to return to the flat you bought with your friend, yet return to it alone. She's busy being happy with her boyfriend, which means you will eat your tea with no company.

Maybe you'll post a picture of that tea online. Or a selfie of you all cuddled up looking cute in your pyjamas. Or of your feet in front of the TV as you post about a nice evening watching Netflix.

Because then you'll get lots of likes.

And those likes will make it seem as if someone wants the

life you portray. As if they envy the woman you are, the world you've built for yourself.

Anyone can envy what they don't have, Stella.

Hell, you envy it. You are jealous of this life you present. Of this world you never actually built.

But that is why you need that validation, and I get that now.

And suddenly I find myself falling in love with you even more.

Here, I thought you were just attention-seeking.

But no more, Stella. No more.

I can see it now.

You aren't damaged. You are lost.

You aren't broken. You're just missing a spare part.

I can be that spare part, Stella.

Really, I can.

And, when I pull up outside your flat, and I see you standing solemnly by the window, leaning your head against the glass, I know you won't pick up my call.

But I also know this is a perfect opportunity to make you need me.

So I put my phone to the ear, and I see you lift your phone, and you don't divert me. That would make it obvious. You just put it down, let it ring out, and your answer phone talks to me.

"Hey you, this is Stella, I can't answer your call right now, so leave a message and, if I feel like it, I might just think about calling you back."

Even your answer phone message is this wondrous ball of fun you want everyone to think you are.

Like I said, I don't think it's sad anymore.

But I don't find it endearing either.

"Hey, this is — it's Noah. I'm not cancelling tomorrow or anything, it's just… This may sound weird, and I really know it does, I just, I had this sense that you maybe weren't feeling great. I don't know how or why, and I know I sound a bit farfetched or, I don't know, strange, please don't get freaked out. I… well, I just wanted to tell you I think you're awesome. I think you're gorgeous. And I can't wait until tomorrow. And if you are feeling down, then – please don't. Because you don't deserve to feel bad. So, er… this is the weirdest message I've left, I get that, I just… I don't know. I wanted you to know. See you tomorrow night, I guess."

I hang up.

You'll love this, I know you will.

You want to believe in fate and soulmates. You like the idea of it. Something wishy-washy and dreamy that will make you feel you're in one of those romance movies you watch so avidly.

Your phone rings. It's your answer phone.

You glare at it.

Maybe you think it's me cancelling.

Reluctantly, you listen.

And, as you listen, I see that smile.

It grows. Lengthens the more you listen, the more you love me.

When it's done, you're just holding the phone by your lap, smiling to yourself, content, happy.

That was exactly what you needed to hear.

And I somehow knew that.

You loved it. I can see that.

You are so pleased you may have found someone who could live up to the dream.

Is that what I have to be, to stop your boredom? A dream?

I don't know how long I can sustain that, but I'll try, really, I will.

You type something. Seconds later, my phone bleeps.

You have sent me a text message.

Thanks, Noah. You were right... Just what I needed to hear... Can't wait to see you tomorrow X X

Two kisses. Oh my, I haven't seen them before.

But it's not the kisses that draw my attention.

You didn't say looking forward to seeing me, you didn't say you will see me — you said *can't wait.*

You probably regret that now. It's over eager. To you, anyway.

But I like it.

You disappear from the window.

Minutes later a picture is on Facebook. Of a glass of wine. A bowl of pasta. A book, I can't quite tell which one, but it's a scruffy book, one that you've read many times.

The caption reads:

Guess it's not all that bad #lifeisforliving #baddaymadebetter

It's a post about me. I don't like my life being broadcast over social media, but it makes me happy, I guess — because it's your version of expression. It's the way you deal with happiness. The way you have to let everyone know.

I leave.

I need a good night's sleep.

Because it's tomorrow now, Stella. It's tomorrow.

And I want to be ready for you.

12

STELLA

IT MEANS EVERYTHING.

He doesn't know it, but this changed my world.

Normally I look out my window at constellations of stars and feel insignificant, but now, it doesn't feel so bad; like being insignificant is okay. Because that means there's no purpose, and if there is no reason to anything, then I can just enjoy living without worrying.

It's dramatic.

I know it is.

But maybe there is a reason to him, even if there is no reason to me. Maybe he came for a reason, like he was sent.

I mean, to be able to just sense, after not even knowing me, that my day was as terrible as it was…

How did he do that? How did he know to say the exact right thing at the exact right time?

I didn't think guys like that even existed.

But he does.

He doesn't care about games and whether he's overeager — he just lives. Just does what he wants, when he knows it's right. Including checking that a woman he just met is okay because his gut tells him she isn't.

That guy in the café… I was beginning to think that's all guys were. Just people who will tell me what I want to hear so they can find out what it's like to fuck me.

Guys don't think about commitment. About feelings. About my thoughts. Guys have never cared about making me happy.

Then again, is it that guys never cared — or they just can't understand how to make me feel content?

I read that male and female brains are different and we shouldn't expect to understand each other. That we should just accept our lover as they are.

I am so *tired* of just accepting what I get.

But with Noah…

He's different.

It's as if destiny brought him to me.

He's not just some guy off Tinder, or some weirdo from the gym.

He's a guy who sits in the café and reads Dickens. He's the guy who knows when he needs to check if I'm okay and is not afraid to do so.

He's the guy who fate has brought to me.

Ah, there's that word.

Fate.

The actual F word that people dread using.

But it must be fate, otherwise how would someone like this find me?

Fate directed him into the café, and directed me to take his order, and directed him to say exactly what I believe about those two books.

The universe engineered it so our worlds would collide and we would fall in love and we would grow old in each other's arms.

He checked if I was okay.
Because of a feeling.
A hunch.
How does that even happen?
I told you, Stella.
Ah, yes. Fate.
Could it be that I have found my soulmate?

13
NOAH

I DON'T BELIEVE IN SOULMATES.

Ridiculous idea, really. That, with a population of seven billion in the world, two people that are meant to be together will miraculously find each other, is a pathetic idea.

Even the most ardent, passionate of romantics shouldn't be so foolish.

Besides, it's insulting.

To be someone's soulmate, to be destined to be the one, suggests you have to stay together because it's set out by the universe, and they are the only one for you.

Whereas, if you admit that there could be many people for you, but you make it work with one person despite there being many others you could be with, that is really special.

To be with a person because you want to, when you could have a vast array of suitors — that is love.

Not anything to do with the ridiculous notion of fate.

But I bet Stella doesn't see it that way.

I bet she's already deducing I could be *the one.*

Which is a stupid idea.

But I'll go along with it, Stella.

For you.

Because I want to be with you, and sometimes that means going along with your wayward ideas, however nonsensical they are.

People get so uptight when challenged about this stuff.

If I dare be a sceptic and voice an opinion, it's like I'm shattering the entire world of vulnerable fools who are desperate to believe in anything that will add some magic to the magically diminishing purpose of life.

I'm here. It's fleeting. Then I'm done.

No heaven and no hell.

I didn't exist for so many years before, why care if I don't exist for so many years again?

We need not conjure fairies to bring magic to the world. Just lower your perception of what magic is.

But you're not like that, are you, Stella?

You need to believe in something greater; you need to attach meaning to the meaningless, otherwise you will struggle to find the point in living.

There has to be a grand design to your life, like the reasons for your pain will expose themselves and suddenly, one day, you will Disney your life into a happy ending.

That's why it will be so easy to get you to attach yourself to me.

Because I needn't give you anything but meaning; that Disney prince, that happy ending; something that dulls the monotony and allows you to pretend for another day that reason and logic exist in life – when it just doesn't.

But you need to believe it does.

And, well, I guess that's okay.

It will have to be.

Because I must go our entire lives without challenging it, just so you can keep peace in your mind.

If you entertained my notion of a meaningless, chaotic

life, then it would bring meaningless chaos into your mind; it's a concept you cannot cope with.

If you believed what I believed, you wouldn't be able to live with it.

If I believed what you believed, I'd be miserable that I had to spend every day according to the plan set out for me.

I live my life without right or wrong, without a correct or incorrect decision, without organisation to the anarchy of our minds.

I live it hoping to be yours, for what that is worth, and finding enough meaning in the simple action of having you in my arms and knowing that you belong there, and will stay there, despite the chaos and anarchy thrown our way.

But you can attribute purpose to these events if you have to, Stella. If it helps you cope.

Honestly, if you weren't so miserable you wouldn't need to.

Maybe after I wipe the misery from your being, you will no longer need such extreme beliefs.

All you will need is me.

And that is how it should be.

14
STELLA

Today's the day.

As fortune or fate would have it, my shift ends a few hours earlier than normal. Meaning I have the many hours it takes to get ready laid out before me.

The first decision is what to wear.

We are going for drinks. The place is Mannie's Wine Bar. It's classy, but not that classy. It's presented well, but the clientele aren't particularly fancy. So if I underdress, I won't meet the demands of the place, yet if I overdress, I will stand out from everyone else there — in a way that I do not wish to, I mean. I want to stand out so he looks at me above everyone else, but because he thinks I look good, not because I look out of place.

I wish I knew what he was wearing. Then I'd at least be able to match his level of classiness.

If I show up in a snazzy dress and he's wearing t-shirt and jeans, that would be the worst ever.

Similarly, if I show up in a casual skirt and a casual blouse and he's there in smart trousers and a shirt, I would feel so foolish.

I sift through my wardrobe. Considering I have so many dresses, it seems bizarre that I can't find a single one I wish to wear.

The only thing I can do is bring out the potentials. I go through them and, on the third time of looking, I pick out a red dress. It's dark red, so it's not in-your-face red, but it has a slight slit above the waist that adds a layer of sluttiness.

It's a hot dress, but what if it's too slutty for him? Will he look at me and think *wow she looks fit in that dress,* or will he look at me and think *did not know I was dating a slag...*

I place it on the bed and keep looking. I remove a blue dress as well, a long one. It has a slit, but it's up the side of the leg, so it's not as revealing as the red dress. It's a sexy dress, but it feels like more of a ball gown, and I will undoubtedly stick out in the wrong way.

I pull out a green dress. It's fitted, stops halfway down my thigh, and allows a slight tease of cleavage. Only problem is, I bought it when I was slightly bigger, and I don't know if it will fit.

This decision can wait. I conclude that standing here, mulling over the choices of dress, is doing nothing but taking up time I could use to get ready.

I put *Radio 1* on and march to the shower. I listen to the drive-time show and even sway my hips to a few tunes. I allow the water to cascade over me, so hot it turns my skin red, and wash every strand of my hair.

Twenty minutes later I emerge, a towel around my body. I check the clock. I have two hours, which should be enough time for my hair to dry on its own — it always looks best when it has that bit of fluffiness it gets when it dries naturally. I can use a towel or a hairdryer if I'm in a hurry, but it will lack that extra bounce.

I singalong to Titanium, making up the words I don't

know, and I paint my nails. I go with a dark red, coating every toe and finger with a swift flick of the brush.

Next, the lingerie.

Now, I need to decide. Am I going to be honest with myself?

I wish to wear sexy lingerie. But is that because I wish for him to see it tonight?

Of course I do, but I also long to have the willpower to wait.

I don't want to be a first date kind of girl, but I know that my history dictates that I am. However much I convince myself I'll wait, I also want to be prepared in case I do not manage to preserve those principles I have never preserved before.

Fuck it.

Wearing sexy lingerie makes me feel good about myself, whether or not someone sees it. Knowing I have this waiting beneath my clothes will give me that extra push of confidence I need.

I pick out a red lace bra and thong that match my nails and slide into them.

I look in the mirror.

I look good.

I hate every part of my body, but if I position myself in just the way so I can't see the cellulite on my buttocks, or the scars on my thighs, or the rolls that inevitably appear when I bend over despite my size eight body, then I can just about believe it — I could be sexy.

I mull over the dresses.

The green dress it is.

Yes, it's a size ten, a size above my size, and it's a little big, but it's the best option. Besides, it pushes my tits up in a way that means he will not miss them.

Next, make-up.

I apply the foundation first, then the mascara, then the eyeliner, then the lippy.

The clock tells me I'm only running ten minutes late.

Personal record.

I get up to go, then I remember — shoes.

I still need to pick my shoes.

Dammit.

15
NOAH

Five minutes until I need to go.

I have a quick shower, put on a nice shirt, a pair of jeans, some smart brown shoes, and I leave.

16
STELLA

I'M TWENTY MINUTES LATE WHEN MY TAXI FINALLY PULLS UP. I can see him outside Mannie's Wine Bar, checking his watch and tapping his foot.

He wears a nice shirt and a smart pair of jeans. Smart shoes, too. I will not look too overdressed next to him, which is perfect.

I approach him, ready to apologise profusely for my lateness, but I don't. After all, it's dating decorum, isn't it? No one ever turns up on time, do they? I bet he's only just arrived himself.

God knows I don't want him to know how keen I am.

As I walk toward him, I make believe I'm walking down the aisle, my hand on my father's arm, and as he turns around and smiles at me, I almost feel it's real.

"You made it," he says, and I can tell he is hiding a bit of irritation at my lateness. Fair play to him though, he hides it well.

"Yes," I say, then awkwardly think of something else to add. "How are you?"

"Thirsty," he says, and he holds out his arm. "Shall we?"

He smiles that smile. It's a cheeky yet warm smile, I hope he shows me that smile as we make love.

We enter the wine bar and I ask for a small glass of red, but he says "nonsense!" and orders an entire bottle.

He walks me to a seat he had reserved — so forward thinking, so organised, so unlike me; I love it — and he pours my glass of wine before he pours his own.

He's being a gentleman, but I feel like he's doing it without being a chauvinist. Something so few men can achieve.

"So, Stella," he says. "Tell me about your favourite book."

His smile twinkles at me, and I can't help but smile in return. I love it. His conversation is already perfect. No mundane chat about the weather, no idle conversation about whether I got here okay, what the traffic was like, not even asking me how I am — just straight into the stuff that matters. My favourite book.

"I feel embarrassed to say it," I admit.

"Nonsense. Embarrassment be damned. How about I tell you mine first?"

"Okay."

He takes in a big deep breath, looks around as if he's hiding a secret, and leans in close. He waves me closer and I can't help but lean in toward him.

He smells good.

"Danny the Champion of the World."

I take a moment to recall this book, but when I do, I can't help but be impressed, and I stick out my bottom lip to indicate as such.

"Roald Dahl," I observe.

"I know it's a kid's book, but I read it about three times a year. My dad used to read it to me when I was a kid, and it just seems comforting. It's such a strange book, though."

"How so?"

"Well, it's just about a kid who helps his dad catch a bunch of pheasants. Not a gripping premise. But really, it's gripping."

"I'm impressed."

"So, now I've suffered the humiliation of revealing I still read a children's book, how about you tell me yours?" He leans in again. "You can whisper it to me if you wish."

17

NOAH

IT REALLY PISSES ME OFF THAT SHE'S LATE.

It's as if my time isn't worth a damn. As if the minutes of my life matter so little that it doesn't matter if she wastes them.

I almost don't even pay attention to the fact that she looks stunning, or that she smiles as she approaches me, or that the curves of her slim, perfect body are outlined succinctly by that dress.

She may be a knockout, but she was late.

I *hate* tardiness.

There is no excuse for being late. If you might be twenty minutes late, then begin preparations twenty minutes earlier. Plan your outfit the night before if you need to.

She doesn't even apologise. In fact, she does not even acknowledge it. I showed up here five minutes early, hoping it would mean we get an extra five minutes together, and here you are, climbing out of a taxi as if it was the driver's fault.

I force a smile.

I know I need to get over this, but I take a while to do so.

Once I have ordered the wine and we have found our booth and we have sat down, I have buried my annoyance, and I can finally engage with her as if she was a person worthy of my conversation.

I ask her what her favourite book is. I know she'll love this. None of the bullshit conversations you share in the awkwardness of bullshit talking — she is a self-confessed literature nerd, and even though I know this is mostly appearance and she has read very little literary fiction, I know she will love this opener.

Still, the more I talk to her the more I get annoyed by her being late. It feels like something I can't get over.

I talk about my favourite book, and it seems to distract my pre-occupied mind.

"So, now I've suffered the humiliation of revealing I still read a children's book, how about you tell me yours?"

I lean in closer, knowing she will love this, as if we are sharing a secret, and she feels all the more intimate with me because of it.

"You can whisper it to me if you wish."

She creates this big performance about preparing herself. She takes in a deep breath, composes, smiles, opens her mouth — the inconsiderate bitch was late — then she speaks.

"Twilight."

Oh dear God, how could this get any worse?

Not only did she waste twenty minutes of my life, she has now wasted all the time I spent working on her beforehand.

It did not say this anywhere on her profile. If it had, I would have ended my pursuit then and there.

"You look disgusted by that," she observes, and I see a flutter of concern dance across her face. She's worried she's said the wrong thing.

Which you have, Stella. The very wrong thing.

I try to deal with it.

It's fine, it's only one setback.

I just hate that fucking book.

It is a deplorable book.

It is everything wrong with young adult teenage-girl-wanking-over-their-fantasy fiction.

"It's… not my favourite," I admit, saying it lightly.

"I mean, I know it's not everyone's favourite, but… I loved it as a teenager."

Of course you did.

The main character is a personalityless, grumpy, never-smiling, never-having-fun, self-obsessed, teenage brat. Every teenage girl can relate to her. That is why they read it.

And, because two men are fighting over this character, it convinces the reader that maybe two men will fight over them; despite them also being a personalityless, grumpy, never-smiling, never-having-fun, self-obsessed, teenage brat.

And the movies…

How many times did that werewolf dickhead run around topless? No girl gives a shit about the story. They just want to finger themselves over the topless horde of pricks.

And, most importantly, and I really, truly stress this — vampires do not sparkle.

I repeat.

Vampires. *Do not.* Sparkle.

"I take it you don't like Twilight?" she asks.

"You could say that."

She looks timid. Put out. Like her cat just died.

And I feel something else die.

My passion. My determination. My vehement obsession with you, Stella, is dying.

"It's fine," she says. "Why don't we talk about something else?"

Oh, yes, Stella. Let's talk about something else.

Your profile said you like great pieces of music.

Let's talk about that, and you can share the pretentious crap that hides the fact you only show interest in what makes you *look* interesting.

You pretend to like great works of literature, then you strum yourself to fucking Twilight.

You are a joke.

Part of a fake image you present to hide how very, truly boring you actually are.

This is why men just fuck you and leave you, Stella. Because that's all you offer them. A fading, attractive body that a man would only want to use once.

You're like a dog-shit bag; it serves its purpose, then you dispose of the vile contents.

"What music do you like?" I ask.

"Classical."

Ah, of course.

I wish to probe further. Perhaps you appreciate *Adagio in G Minor?* Or is *Requiem in D Minor* more your kind of thing? Or what about Bach's masterpieces? *Das Wohltemperierte Klavier I: Prelude and Fugue No. 1 in C Major* perhaps?

"Ah, what is your favourite?"

"I love Hall of the Mountain King."

Oh dear sweet Jesus.

It is not called *Hall of the Mountain King*; it is in fact *Suite No. 1 Op 46* from the play, *Peer Gynt,* composed by Edvard Grieg.

But for most people, it is just the soundtrack to an old Alton Towers advert.

I humour you.

"Do you like anything else by Edvard Grieg?"

"Who?"

Fucking Jesus, you are a dumb shit.

I feel like I'm testing you, Stella.

Testing to call out your bullshit.

What else do you pretend?

How else do you present this image of fake sophistication?

This is your problem, Stella.

I wanted to be the one you thought was your soulmate. I wanted to be your destiny, the last relationship you ever had.

But, like every other guy you've dated, after getting to know you just a little, I can see the truth.

That all you're worth is a fuck.

You'll be disappointed when I dodge your calls.

You'll wonder why you did it again.

Why you let yourself believe, only to be fooled.

Sorry, Stella.

I will play the game tonight.

I will say the things I know you want to hear.

I will go along with your bullshit, just so I can see you naked, and I can thrust myself into you until you scream.

Then I'll be gone.

You aren't worth what I thought you were.

18
STELLA

He's perfect.

He accepts my lateness, and he knows how to engage in conversation in a way other men just can't.

He talks to me about literature.

About classical music.

I can't help getting carried away. I don't know what is wrong with me... It's our first date and already I'm picturing us on our deathbed, holding hands, talking about the wonderful life we've led. I've already picked my maid of honour, I already know the perfect place for us to get married, and I already know what you'll say in your speech.

You want two kids. A boy and a girl. And a dog — not a big dog. Maybe a terrier, or a sausage dog.

You want to move to the country to raise them. Find a pleasant cottage or a bungalow to live. Somewhere with a real fireplace we can gather around to keep warm in the winter. Somewhere we can take walks in the summer.

You are telling me everything I want to hear, and I can't help but picture it all happening with you.

You ask me what I want in my future, and the answer, Noah, the answer is *you.*

Everything you've just said is perfect.

Everything you offer me is perfect.

Let's do it.

Let's get married. Let's get carried away. Let's meet our parents and quit our jobs and live a poor life, but a full one.

I don't notice the wine bottle going down. He refills my glass before he refills his every time.

A few hours later, the barman announces last orders.

He asks if he can walk me home.

I say it's a half-hour walk.

He says he doesn't care, so long as he gets to spend that half-hour holding my hand.

A man that wants to hold my hand…

Normally I have to force it. No man ever wants public displays of affection. As if they are ashamed to be with me, as if they don't want people to know.

But Noah does.

He wants the entire world to know I'm his girl.

And I am, you know.

Completely, totally, and utterly.

I forget this is our first date.

I forget this is too early.

I allow myself to get carried away as, in his eyes, I can see him getting carried away too.

He gives me his coat and keeps his arm around me. It's not that cold, but I don't object.

We reach my flat building.

He looks at me, and he leans in, and his lips meet mine, and they touch so delicately at first, then sink into it, deeper, harder, and the words escape my lips in a whisper before I have any idea I've said them.

"Would you like to come up?"

He doesn't answer at first. He kisses me again, as if he's thinking about it, but he need not think about it.

"Do you even have to ask?" he says, so quietly only I can hear him, and it's like we have our own little world, and I am already in love.

I open the door, and we giggle all the way up the stairs.

19

NOAH

She's not a great fuck.

She does the job, don't get me wrong.

But I spend at least fifteen minutes going down on her, then she begs me to fuck her. Sorry, darling, but I need a little warming up too.

She says, "Do you not want to?"

Yes, I do. But you need to suck my cock first.

I warmed you up; you warm me up. It's how it works.

So I don't even ask.

I move my body over her lying body, and I place the tip against her lips. She looks surprised, and doesn't open her mouth.

I hold her nose. Her mouth opens and in I go.

She tries to say something but I don't give a fuck.

After five minutes, I'm ready.

I slide inside.

I don't wear a condom.

She doesn't object.

Stupid bitch. I could have anything, and you just let me slide in.

I don't even check you're on the pill, but I assume so. I don't really care, to be honest.

Condoms do nothing but make it worse.

She stares up at me as if she's surprised, and I realise it's just her sex face. I move and she makes no noise, her expression doesn't even change.

I wonder if I'm doing it wrong. Whether she doesn't like it this way.

And I remember I don't care.

I'm not keeping her beyond tonight, so it's not like I need to make sure she enjoys herself.

I turn her over, and I fuck her from behind.

I'm tired of looking at her.

Her arse is perfect. There's cellulite, but that never bothers me. It only bothers me when the woman is so insecure about it she can't cope with being seen naked.

I look around the room as I pound her. She has an excessive amount of teddy bears and a vanity desk covered in makeup. There's also a large slab of wood in the corner of the room, which is strange, as I can't see any other evidence of DIY.

After a while she makes noise, moaning and grunting on each thrust.

I wonder why I care.

I'm getting tired now, so I decide it's time to finish.

I speed up and I scream a masculine roar as I cum.

I don't stay inside of her. I don't stay close. I move away and go to her bathroom, using large clumps of toilet paper to wipe myself off.

When I come out, she's laid on the bed, naked.

She looks like she should be attractive, but she must just dress well. Yes, she's slim. Her breasts are a good size. Her legs curve. She just lacks something.

Pride over her body, perhaps. That confidence that makes a person sexy.

I must have stood here for too long, as she reaches her arms out and tries to usher me back.

"Come back to bed," she says. "I want to cuddle."

A day ago I would have relished this. I would have welcomed this opportunity to hold her in my arms and feel my love grow and feel us get ever closer.

Now I want nothing less.

I look for my underwear.

"I'm going," I say.

"You're going?"

"Yes."

"You can stay if you want."

"I don't."

"But—"

"Where the fuck are my pants?"

I look at her and she looks at me and she looks so wounded, like a battered pup or an abandoned kitten.

"Don't you like me?"

I hesitate.

I hate this part.

"I won't be calling you," I admit

"What? Why?"

I shrug. "Don't think it's going to work."

"Then why did you have sex with me?"

"You invited me up."

"Yes. Because I thought you liked me."

I sigh. I hate this, but the best way is just to be honest.

"I don't."

"You don't?"

"No."

"Why?"

"I think you're pretentious. Insecure. You make yourself out to be something you're not. And I just don't like it."

I find my underwear, finally.

I put it on.

And I look up.

And she's crying.

Fuck's sake.

20
STELLA

I can't help it.

I want to spend my life with him.

I've seen it.

I've been picturing it all evening.

His proposal at the top of a secluded hill in the rain. We won't care it's raining because it's romantic, because our love beats any weather.

Our marriage at the same hotel where my parents married.

Our kids.

Our retirement.

Holding hands forty years into the future because it feels just as special as it did on our first date.

Yet here he is, saying all these hurtful things.

Like he means it.

But he doesn't.

And I hate that I'm crying, but I can't help it.

"Control yourself," he says. "Stop being pathetic."

"I'm not!"

That's not fair, Noah. I am not being pathetic. You're just being unreasonable.

He puts on his trousers.

I take his t-shirt and hold on to it.

He looks everywhere for it. Under the bed, in the sheets around the floor.

Then he sees me holding it.

"Give me my t-shirt," he says blankly.

"No."

"Give it to me."

"Not until you stop saying these things."

"Have some pride, Stella."

"I said to stop saying these things."

"This is why I'm fucking you and leaving you, Stella! Because this is what you're like. You're a fucking psycho."

"I thought you liked me."

"I did."

"Did?"

"You really have no idea who you are, do you?"

He shakes his head.

"You're a sad little girl who pretends she likes literature then quotes her favourite book as Twilight. You say you like classical music and don't even know the composer and actual name of your favourite piece. You're fake. Everything about you is an image you try to create, like you're afraid to just be you. Because, maybe, the real you is boring, and not worth the time. And that is why you have to masquerade as this insincere mess. Guys leave you quickly, Stella, because they see the real you quickly, and it's not what they thought you were. Now, give me my fucking t-shirt."

I stare at him.

Scared.

Still crying.

I don't know why you're saying these things, Noah, I really don't.

Stop lying.

It's not kind.

You hold your hand out.

I give you the t-shirt.

You put it on, followed by your jacket, then pause. Looks at me. Hesitates, as if you have some wisdom you wish to share before you leave my life.

"Get therapy," you tell me. "You need it."

You turn to go.

I can't let you.

I want that proposal. That wedding. That deathbed.

I want it all.

Which is why I pick up the piece of wood.

Which is why I creep up behind you as you reach the door.

Which is why I hit you on the head with it as hard as I can.

You're groggy, so I hit you again. You fall to the floor. I hit you again. And again. And Again.

You lay by my feet, unconscious.

21

NOAH

I WAKE UP, AND IT'S NOT GOOD. I WILL NOT SAY THAT THE sunlight hurts my face, or that the first thing I hear is my breathing, or whatever cliched shit Stella would come out with should she be in my position — but I will say that this situation is completely, totally, and utterly fucked.

I don't want her anymore. I really don't. She isn't what I thought she was. She had potential, but the vapid whore she presents on social media isn't some outward presentation that hides the true gem inside — it is who she is. She isn't inwardly beautiful; she's ugly, both inside and out.

So you can imagine my enormous sigh when I wake up in a cage. How the hell she acquired a cage like this, I don't know — it's almost as if she'd planned it. Like she'd had it prepared. It's a box shape, in a basement. I don't have enough room to stand and I don't have enough room to stretch. I can just sit on the bars below, lean against the bars behind me, then close my eyes and rue the day I met her.

"Hey babe."

In the chaos of my predicament, I had not noticed her outline in the shadows. She sits on a chair, wearing a dress that makes her look a knockout. Normally, this dress would excite me to no end. But it doesn't. It scares me. What is she planning?

She's dressing for more sex.

Does that mean she's going to force me?

"You've been asleep all day, silly," she says. "I was wondering if you would wake up at all. I mean, I've already been to work. Are you comfortable, by the way? Probably not. It's not the best cage, but it's the only way I can be sure that you won't run off somewhere."

I drop my head to the side and stare at her. Why me? Surely there's some idiot out there who could share the kind of mundane conversations the thick have with each other. They could watch daytime television together, enjoying the ravings of an unemployed wino on a trashy talk show with a 50-inch plasma like it means something.

"So what's happening then, Stella?" I ask. "Are you going to force me to fuck you? Then are you going to let me go?"

She chuckles a little. It scares me.

"Let you go?" She stands. "Oh, Noah." She walks toward me. "You are silly."

"We both know this won't work. I don't want to be with you. Just let me go and we're fine, I won't—"

"Enough."

She places her hands on the bars of my cage. She leans in. She smiles, but it's different – I haven't seen her smile like this.

She shakes her head pitifully.

"You think you can overpower me?" I say. "There's no way you can—"

She pulls out some pills. Holds them in her palm.

"Ah," I say. "That's how."

Excuse me for the burden of knowledge, but I know what a roofy looks like.

"And how long are you going to keep this up? You going to let me go or kill me once you're done?"

"Why would I kill you? I love you."

"No, you don't. You love the idea of me. And I do not love you, nor will I ever love you."

She smiles. Nothing deters this girl.

"I don't think you understand," she tells me. "You will love me. We will be happy. For the rest. Of. Our. Lives."

"I'm not—"

"Noah, you can't tell me what you will or will not do anymore. You had that option. I was going to let you love me freely. But you wasted it. Now this is just how it has to be."

She speaks so cheerfully, so resolved. Like she's trying to rationalise with me.

"Please, let me go, Stella. I was just pretending to be who you wanted me to be."

She laughs it off, like I'm being purposefully obtuse. Silly little me! What a fool I am!

"Do you really think I didn't see you outside my flat? You think I didn't stand there purposefully, so you could see me and learn to want me? You think I didn't know you were checking my social media? Please. I've been making you want me from day one. I can make you want me again."

I'm an idiot. A fool. The biggest. And this is what it's done to me.

This is what my life will be now.

"It will take a very, very long time to make me love you, Stella."

She places her hand on mine, giggling when I flinch away.

"Oh, Noah, don't you worry. We've got all the time in the world. You are never leaving me again."

She latches onto my eyes with hers with a happy deadness. I tremble as she runs a hand down my cheek and says the words that act as the figurative nail on my ever-expanding coffin.

"You are going to stay here with me."

She stands. Walks to the door.

"Forever."

She goes to leave, turning out the lights and locking the door as she does.

And, as I sit in the darkness, I sum up my predicament with one perfectly timed word:

"... Fuck."

Roses are red
As you're suggesting
Look at these violets
While I rip out your INTESTINE

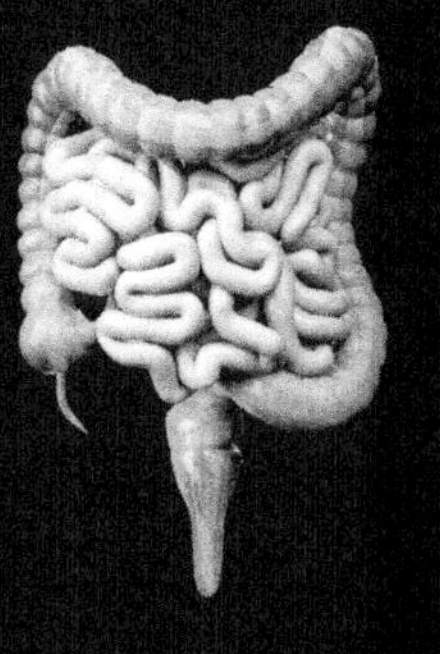

IN SICKNESS AND IN MURDER

LETTER #106

Dear my troubled victim,

I've been watching you, and I feel sorry for you.

You're a mother, but even your own child won't admit to being your son.

When did you stop being a woman? When did having a child become the entirety of your personality? When did you lose everything about who you are?

At work, all you talk about is little Jamie, what he does, and what he's said. People listen with their mouths shut, but you know what they are all thinking: Doesn't this bitch have something else to talk about?

Sometimes you share memories on Facebook of your early twenties. You were thinner, and with better skin, standing next to your best friend in a nightclub. You barely see her now you're both consumed by motherhood. You say you don't talk much anymore because life gets in the way, but that's nonsense — the truth is, she makes you feel like a bad mother. She always arrives on time, with her child behaving impeccably, and home-made sandwiches perfectly prepared for the picnic — whilst you sit there with a screeching toddler and an egg and cress sandwich bought from the local pound shop.

What's worse is that, in those pictures of memories on Facebook, you are the good-looking one — but she has since overtaken you. She looks like she's never even had a child, and you do not understand how she does it, but witnessing the way men check her out in the park and ignore you is just too difficult to take.

Yet you share these pictures. You tag your friend and say something like 'how were we so young' or 'remember what life was like.' You say you've outgrown clubbing because it's what your husband wants to hear, but really, you would love to be on that dance floor with a handsome man you don't know dancing behind you while you gyrate your arse against his crotch.

You fantasise about so many men other than your husband that you're not even sure if you're attracted to him anymore. In fact, you fancy that guy who runs the aerobics class at your gym so much that he has become the reason you pay forty pounds a month for a gym membership you don't otherwise use. You tell your husband you love him and you look him in the eyes on those rare nights he ploughs your absent body, but you aren't looking at him, not really. Yes, you stare up at him enough so he's convinced, but the only way you can cum is by pretending he's someone else.

But you're with him for life. You celebrate anniversaries and give him a card that tells him how great your life is since you found him, how lucky you are, but in truth, he is safe. He is a good guy but you, like most women, are attracted to arseholes.

You don't want a man who will open doors for you and reassure you when you're sad or be a good father to your baby. You want someone who will wreck your life and fuck your best friend and somehow make you still come back.

Your fantasies are the only place where you do not indulge in denial. In this way, you are becoming more and more like your adulterous mother.

Oh, how you despise your mother and the passing comments

about your daughter. Things like, "So you chose to dress her in that colour then?" or "Would you like one of my brushes so you can keep her hair tidy?" You pretend it's nothing, then cry when your husband's asleep.

Everything she says is said with middle class white privilege and a snotty upturned nose, like she has to pretend she is posher than she is.

But do you know what the saddest thing is? Without your mother's company, you would be truly alone.

The only break you get from being a wife, and the only break you get from the constant tyranny of parenthood, is the few hours you spend at your mother's, when she can occupy your child and allow you a moment's rest.

Your profile picture on Facebook is of your child.

You claim this is out of love, but you know that no one likes people who put a picture of their child on their own as their profile picture. Truth is, you can't find a picture of yourself that you like. Every picture you find repulses you. You try to smile but you look at the picture and think — gosh, is that my smile? Is that really what I look like?

Your husband tells you it's a nice picture and, although that's meant to make you feel better, it makes you feel worse, because if that picture is an accurate likeness of how you appear then, fuck, you must be ugly.

How much worse will you look as you get older?

This is why, despite only just turning thirty-two, you apply anti-wrinkle cream. It's not because you have wrinkles, but because your mother suggested you start taking it to prevent you getting wrinkles as you grow older.

You hate that you do it, but your mother knows just which insecurity to prod and poke.

But it's fine. It doesn't matter. Tomorrow, you will go back to your job — which is only part-time, of course. Your husband thinks it best you don't go back to work full-time so you are there for your child; despite him still being allowed a fledging career, it is you who had to give up aspirations in a job you loved.

And, when you get to work, you will show everyone the latest picture of your kid on your phone.

But they know what he looks like.

They just don't care.

But what else do you talk about?

It's all you are, after all.

Yours sincerely,

Henry.

1
SHEILA

THE WAITRESS BRINGS OVER OUR SCONES, AND I GIVE HER AS big a smile as I can.

It's not a pleasant job, let's be honest. Having to deal with people all day, with their complaints and their moaning, it must be rather difficult. Which is why I always ensure I thank a waitress most profusely.

So, as she settles the plates down in front of me, then in front of my dear husband, Henry, I make sure to catch her eye, and spread my smile as wide as I can spread it.

"Thank you ever so much, dear," I say, and she smiles back, and I really do hope I made her day.

Henry doesn't touch his scone. He has his notepad open, and he's writing something. His eyes are fixed on a woman at the cash machine across the street who ignores her screaming child. The woman looks downtrodden and, honestly, I didn't think she would be his type.

"Are you okay, honey?" I ask.

He nods, but he's concentrating.

When he gets in one of these trances, you see, there is

little you can do to break him out of it. You just have to let him ride it out. Let him play out his sordid actions in his mind, craft his next moves, thinking things he thinks I don't know about.

I take the option of low-fat butter. I slice open my scone with a knife and spread the butter evenly on both slices. I take the raspberry jam and spread that. The scone crumbles a bit, but that's okay. I then take the clotted cream and make sure to leave plenty of it for Henry.

"Are you not hungry?"

He grunts a response. Not in a horrible way, but in a way that shows he's acknowledged I've spoken, but he needs to write. When his pen starts moving and the cogs of his brain start whirring, there is little I can do to distract him. Marriage is like the tides of the sea – you have to ride the waves to reach the shore.

As I take the first bite of my scone and delight in its soft texture and the sweetness of the cream — I really do like cream — I notice a child staring at me.

He seems to have paused a few steps away from the table. His mother is engrossed in her phone, texting or what not.

I put my scone down and wave.

"Hello there," I say, using the friendliest, most endearing voice I have. "What's your name?"

He hesitates, then answers.

"Roger."

"Well, it is so very lovely to meet you, Roger!" I point at the toy in his hand. "Who's that?"

"Flug."

"Flug? Why, what a wonderful name."

He picks his lip. A habit I don't particularly like, but one that does not put me off engaging with this delightful child.

The mother lifts her head and realises she does not know where her child is. She turns and sees him talking to me.

"Roger!" she says. "I am ever so sorry."

"Oh, not at all, he was a delight to talk to. A spritely, lovely child."

The mother smiles awkwardly and leads Roger away by the arm.

I turn back to Henry.

He is a kind husband, ageing but dignified about it. Grey hair, not bald. Quiet, rarely says much, but in his silence is where I find his love. It is where I find his affection, and all the words that are left unsaid.

His face rarely flickers with a smile or a grimace. It remains still, unyielding to his environment. He's not easily affected by things, you see. He likes to concentrate on the moment he's in.

He gave up teaching to own a toy shop — before we retired, that is. The children used to delight in running around the shelves adorned with playthings. He never interacted with them much, as he had a manager he employed to put on an enthusiastic voice and engage with all the children. He just liked to stand and watch them play. He would be expressionless, but I could tell he was relishing the joy he brought them.

His sex is rarely passionate, but it's firm and its real. I don't mind missing out on some spontaneity and eagerness one might have in their youth. He looks me in the eyes as he makes love, and that's enough for me.

He is caring.

He is sweet.

He is a good man.

He finishes what he's writing and folds it up.

He thinks I don't know what's on there and what it means, but I do.

"I'll be right back," he says without looking at me, and walks toward the woman he was staring at.

I watch him go. This lady won't know what's coming.

Oh, sorry, I almost forgot — he also likes to deliver letters to women before he murders them.

Didn't I mention?

2

SHEILA

I SIT AT HOME AND KNIT WHILE I WATCH CORONATION STREET. There's another killer or something, and everyone is worried. It's rather farfetched, but I enjoy it, and it passes the time until Henry gets home.

When he gets home, I feel like jumping to my feet and rushing to greet him like a keen little puppy. But I hold myself back. Henry doesn't like it when I do that, he says it suffocates him, so I stay seated.

The front door closes. A minute later, he walks into the living room. His eyes are robotic, staring ahead, widened. His face is expressionless. His body stiff.

He sits on the edge of the sofa and stares at the fireplace.

"Are you all right, dear?" I ask.

He grunts and nods the slightest nod.

He has not done a good job of cleaning himself up.

His shirt is scruffy, like it has been washed but not ironed. His trousers appear to be inside out. The few hairs left on his head stick up.

But it's his hands that are the most incriminating. Her blood is still stuck in his fingernails.

I tut, and I turn the television off.

"Are you going to go in the shower?" I ask.

He doesn't break out of his trance.

"Henry, I really do think you should go in the shower."

Nothing.

"Henry!"

He finally turns to me.

"Shower, please!"

He vacantly nods, stands, and walks rigidly out of the room.

While he showers — he tends to take long showers after he's murdered someone, so I have plenty of time — I walk to the cupboard under the sink, collect the items I need, and check them off as I collect them.

Rubber gloves — check.

Carpet cleaner — check.

Bleach — check.

Sponges — check.

Douche — check.

I enter the garage and close the door. I can't let any neighbours see.

I collect the wheelbarrow and open the car boot.

There she is.

The woman from outside the hairdressers.

She makes an even uglier corpse.

I put the rubber gloves on and get to work.

First thing I do is take the woman out of the boot. She isn't too fat, but that doesn't matter — all dead bodies are heavy. I put my arm under her neck and under her knees. With an "eek!" I hoist her up and shove her in the wheelbarrow.

Boy, that took a bit of effort. I'm not getting any younger, you know. This was far easier when we were twenty-two.

I take the carpet cleaner and spray the bottom of the car

boot. Next, I scrub with the bleach at all the non-carpet areas of the car. I am very thorough, and this takes me more than an hour. I end up exhausted, and quite in need of a shower myself.

Next, I take the douche. I spread the woman's legs.

Yep, just as I suspected. His semen is still leaking out. Silly man, I wish he would not leave such a mess.

I splash some bleach on the douche, widen her legs further, and push it in. It takes a bit of forcing as her body is really quite stiff, and there is no moisture left. However, this is not, as they say, my first rodeo — so I manage after a few hefty pushes.

I twist and push and pull and ensure I have every bit out.

Then, once it is done, I check the neighbours aren't looking and wheel her into the back garden, stopping under the large willow tree that shields me from the neighbour's prying eyes.

I bury her next to that hideous woman with the lip ring who worked at the florists.

When I arrive back in the house, Henry is sitting at the table with a knife and fork in his hands and an empty plate.

"Oh, I am ever so sorry," I say. "I forgot to do your tea, didn't I?"

I am ever so forgetful sometimes!

"What would you like?"

"Beans."

"Anything with them?"

"Toast."

"How many pieces?"

"Two."

"Right you are."

I kiss his forehead and I make my way into the kitchen, preparing the saucepan and the toaster.

I love this man very much.

We all have to deal with the faults of our lovers. Some are jealous, some are possessive, and some are controlling — but not my Henry. He lets me be myself. I really did get lucky.

He just has this one minor fault.

I'm not sure if he realises how much I clear up after him, but I am happy to do it.

Because I am such a lucky, lucky woman.

I think about this as I make his dinner.

Then I notice something…

He's staring out the window at our neighbour's twenty-one-year-old daughter, writing another letter.

LETTER #107

Dear Beautiful Mess,

You're the kind of woman who thinks people hate you because they're jealous, and not because you're a total bitch.

You say you don't want kids because you want to focus on your career, but you don't even know if the career you're in is the career you want. The truth is that you don't want to lose your body, as being thin and mildly attractive is the only thing you feel you can offer someone, so you get a dog you treat like a child instead. You think the dog is cute but even the most passionate of dog lovers would think the yappy little rat is repulsive.

You wake up earlier than you need to put on too much makeup.

You scoff when you think a guy is perving over you and feel shit when they don't.

You say you like chivalry but hate chauvinism, and that belief sums you up — the two are mutually exclusive.

You take pictures of your food for social media; not because it looks good, but to show off how little you eat so everyone is aware of the eating disorder you convince yourself you have.

You don't have one. You just want one. Like having to endure pain might validate you. You just don't want to admit you're as ugly outside as you are in.

Your attention span for men is short, and you love it when they see you as a project, like it gets you off that they think they can turn you into something better. As soon as they verbalise an astute observation about the person you really are, you banish them for the truth and sign up to whatever dating site appears first in the Google search results.

You are most attracted to pricks who treat you like dirt. You fuck them then complain to your male friend about how there are no nice guys for you to date, despite him being a genuinely nice guy who cares about you.

You say you're confident, but your insecurities drive almost every action you take, like how you hold your hair beneath your chin to cover your neck when you take a selfie, and pout your lips because you think it makes your cheekbones look better.

You struggle to scroll down your Facebook feed because of the size of your nails constantly tapping the screen, and they are stupid nails, they really are. You once aspired to be a beautician as your elitist mother taught you that beauty is a woman's worth. As a child, you used to stare at other families playing in the park while your mother bought herself new clothes with her husband's credit card. Now you have no idea what to do with your life. Your values may have changed, but your environment has not.

You never message first on Tinder. If a friendly guy says hello, you taunt them for being uncreative with their opener and unmatch them before they can retort — again, complaining about how you only end up with pricks who treat you like dirt.

You tell guys you don't fuck on the first date, then fuck on the second. You rarely have an orgasm but that's not why you do it, is it? Sure, you get horny, but the knowledge that someone wants to fuck you is what really turns you on. It makes you feel you're worth something.

Until the next day, when he leaves without a number and you feel even worse.

But it's okay, right?

Because no matter how much you hurt, you have drawers full of foundation to cover it up.

And it allows you to convince yourself you're pretty.

So do your hair, style your clothes, and push up the cleavage. That crack between your breasts represents the biggest crack in your facade.

I see you.

I do.

And I can't wait to ruin your life.

3
SHEILA

THESE LETTERS ARE GETTING MORE FREQUENT.

It used to be just once a year. Then it became once every few months, then weeks... now I am expected to clean up within days!

It's unsustainable.

A woman's body shows up in the middle of the garden this time. In the garden!

Not in the garage, not in the car boot, not even hidden in the darn shed — our neighbour's daughter is just there, on an indiscreet patch of grass, for all our neighbours to see!

"Oh, Henry, you silly boy," I say, as I rush to take hold of the woman's legs.

I look upwards, glancing at the windows, checking if anyone is looking. There is one twitchy curtain, but that could just be in my mind.

Either way, I do not have time to dwell on it.

I pull the legs to the back entrance to the garage. Now, I don't know if you have ever tried to pull a dead body along the floor, but just in case you haven't — it is not an easy feat!

A corpse is heavy; far heavier than they were when they were alive. It is entirely dead weight and, by the feel of this woman, rigor mortis has set in, which also makes her quite stiff.

I drag her in, close the door behind me, and lean against the Lamborghini. I take a handkerchief from my sleeve and dab my forehead. I am sweating like nobody's business!

Oh, Henry. You really have made a kerfuffle this time.

I don't have time to dwell. I've bought myself a bit of time by taking this lady into the garage, but I don't have all day – it is well past five now, and Henry will expect his tea at half-past six. I best get moving.

I open my chest of tools, and I move aside the wire cutter, the clamp, and the various utensils I have used over the years, until I find the freshly sharpened axe.

It is silly to try to break up a body by hitting it in the middle of a muscle; it would just be too tough. It's best to use the joints. So I start at the bottom, with the feet, and I hold the axe up high then swing it at the ankle.

It takes a good fifteen to twenty minutes, and a lot of muscle power, for me to reduce the ankle to the last few tendons. It clings on stubbornly, like a spider's web on a speeding car. I feel too old to still be doing this, but I wipe the sweat from my brow and begin work on the knee.

Gosh darn it, this will take a while. I may not get this done before tea-time; I might even have to postpone our evening game of Scrabble. Henry will not be pleased about that.

Today is Friday, and we always treat ourselves to home cooked fish and chips on Friday. I usually batter the fish myself, but I will have to look in the freezer to see if I have any already battered, as I'm not sure I have time. Henry far prefers the home-battered ones, but hopefully he'll understand. I don't like it when he has that look of disappointment on his face. He may not say anything, but I can see when he's disappointed.

I go to the bathroom on the way and wash my hands thoroughly. I enter the kitchen, ready to do what I need to, and something catches my eye.

It is an envelope.

With my name on it, and Henry's handwriting.

And there appears to be a letter inside.

LETTER #108

To my wife,

It has been thirty-four years since we married, and in that time, I have never mentioned my true thoughts. In fact, I have stayed silent on the matter.

But I believe it is time we are honest with each other.

You are not what you once were. When we met, we were just nineteen. Your curves were voluptuous, your skin was immaculate, and your dress sense highlighted all those parts of your body you loved to tease me with.

Now, your body barely has a shape. You claim to have an hourglass figure, but I have never seen an hourglass as distorted and fucked-up as your withering mess.

Your skin is sagging. You have a tattoo of a rose on your ankle you claimed you acquired for me, despite my hatred of people who permanently etch ink upon their flesh. That rose is now wilted and caught in the bumps of hairy meat. You may shave your legs for the rare occasions we still muster the energy for sex, but hairs still poke out of those moles that scatter over your body.

And your dress sense. Oh, how you used to wear such lovely dresses. They would tease me with a bit of thigh beneath your fishnet tights. Now, fishnet tights on your thigh looks more like string wrapped around turkey.

You insist on wearing these silk garments that look like they are taken from a catalogue of Victorian clothing. Your hair is short, white, and curly, which it never was before, and I dislike it. All it does is reveal your neck. I once made your breath quiver by kissing that neck; now its appearance just increases my impotence.

You talk to me without ever getting a reply and never wonder why. You spend evenings and mealtimes just yapping about some nonsense I couldn't care less about. Even through Scrabble, a game that requires concentration, you do not shut your trap.

I could not care less about who has died on Coronation Street. The fact that you watch such an unintellectual, poorly acted diarrhoea of television makes me sickened that I have given you so many years of my life.

This is where it ends, my darling.

You must admit, you have survived many years without repercussions for your foolhardy behaviour. But it is time for me to reveal to you my secret.

This secret may shock you, but that doesn't matter, as you will not be alive much longer after you read it.

Here it is:

I murder people.

Specifically, women. I do not know how I have gotten away with it for so long, but I appear to be quite an astute, nimble killer. I deliver my notes to these women and, shortly after, I take their lives. It began in my twenties, and I have done it my whole life with no reprieve.

Now it is your turn to die and give me the freedom to live out my pension years without your incessant nonsense plaguing my retirement.

Who knows how long I have left? I do not know, and I surely do not wish to waste any more of my life entertaining your infuriating ways.

Goodbye, my dear.

I promise I will make it quick.

4
SHEILA

My hands shake as I read it.

Could this really be?

All that I have done for him, and he has no idea?

I thought he knew. I thought he was aware, if only on a subconscious level, that I have cleared up his mess for all these years.

My love is persistent and holds no prejudice. I have not judged his need to kill. I have not scalded him or exiled him as so many women might. In my wedding vows I said, "In sickness and in health," and gosh darn it, I plan to stick to that.

But now…

I turn to find a shadow looming over me.

"Hello, my dear," he says, the most he's said to me in years.

"Darling," I say.

I turn to run, but there is nowhere to run to. There are no doors I could get to in time.

The oven is on. The fish and chips are in. I wonder if he'll know to take them out after thirty minutes once he is done with me.

He has something in his hand. It looks like a large clock. The one we received from my parents as a wedding present. He uses it to strike me over the head and I collapse on the floor.

The world is blurry. Red covers my vision. I try to blink the blood away, but there is too much of it.

He pounds my skull and my vision goes completely.

He mounts me. I can't see him, but I know how his body feels on top of me.

Another strike and I can only hear his breathing in the distance.

Another strike and I don't even have that.

And, as my life falls out of my body, I try to muster three words that never come.

"I love you..."

I guess this is the way it had to happen.

But, like I said, I meant my marriage vows.

My man has to do what he has to do — and I stand by him in sickness.

In health.

And in murder.

5

HENRY

THE POLICE ARRIVE LATER. SOMETHING ABOUT A NEIGHBOUR seeing a woman dragging a body across my garden.

They find Sheila's body, and they have found our neighbour's body in the garage with her foot hacked off. I'm not quite sure how she lost her foot, as I am fairly sure I did not do that. Either way, I know I'll have no choice but to plead guilty to her murder.

The police erect tape around the house, cordon off the street, and the neighbours stare at me as I sit in the back of the police car. More police arrive and a few minutes later I'm driven away. The whole time, I'm just thinking — I don't understand...

I've never been caught before, why now?

I'll spend the rest of my life in prison, which is annoying.

It was hardly how I'd planned to spend my retirement.

But hey, who knows, maybe there will be someone to play Scrabble with me. I imagine inmate's education levels aren't high, and I'd be able to win easily. None of those pretend wins when Sheila lost deliberately so I wouldn't feel bad.

I would have my own television and not have to endure Coronation Street

And I would not have to listen to her rambling.

I smile.

Maybe it isn't so bad, after all.

Roses are red

Violets aren't green

I'm going to impale you

Then eat your SPLEEN

DEATH OF THE HONEYMOON

[POLICE INTERVIEW TRANSCRIPT]

OFFICER Tell me about the day you met him.

HARRY I've done this.

OFFICER Do it again.

HARRY (sighs) I've already told you.

OFFICER How did you initiate contact?

HARRY On a website.

OFFICER What was the website called?

HARRY Do you not realise what has happened! Why are you treating me like – like – have you not visited the house, seen what… My wife is–

OFFICER Harry, please, just answer the question. We're just trying to get to the bottom of what happened.

HARRY I *told* you what happened. I told your colleague what happened. *At least* three times.

OFFICER Harry, come on. We're trying to help.

HARRY The website, it – it was called Adult Threesome Finder.

OFFICER And what did the website do?

HARRY (pause) Pretty much what it says. It helps hook you up with a third party.

OFFICER For…?

HARRY What do you think? A threesome.

OFFICER And this was your choice?

HARRY Not particularly.

OFFICER So it wasn't consensual?

HARRY Yes, it was consensual.

OFFICER But it wasn't your choice?

HARRY Would you choose to watch another man have sex with your wife?

OFFICER So was there sexual assault?

HARRY No.

OFFICER We found traces of semen on–

HARRY That's not the problem! The sex was not the problem!

OFFICER So you wanted to have sex with him?

HARRY No, and – I did not have sex with him. That is not what worked, not how it happened. This wasn't a *gay* thing, I am not – I – I just want you to help!

OFFICER I'm trying, Harry. It's just, if you're saying there was no sexual assault...

HARRY No, the actual act of, of, of what we met for – that was consensual. It was Lucy's idea.

OFFICER So let me get this straight – you both had sex with her, but there was no sex between you and him.

HARRY No, for Christ's sake. That isn't the problem, that is not what the problem is, that was fine, it – it – it...

OFFICER I'm just really struggling to see what's happened here.

HARRY That's because you're focussing on the wrong thing. It was *him.* He wasn't – he wasn't what we thought he'd be. That came after.

OFFICER After what?

HARRY The... the threesome.

OFFICER So you're saying he didn't hurt you until after he'd had sex with your wife?

HARRY Not exactly.

OFFICER Then what are you saying? Please, help me out here.

HARRY He – he – I… I can't.

OFFICER You can't?

HARRY No.

OFFICER Why not?

HARRY (hesitates) Because of who he was.

1

NOW

To say that this was Harry's first choice would be an extreme inaccuracy. In fact, at one point, this was barely a choice. It was a last resort.

But, like most last resorts, it was there because at some point it will become the *only* resort.

So you could say, with certainty, two definite things about Harry:

1/ This was not his first choice.

2/ He loved Lucy more than anything.

And boy, did he love Lucy. Not just the way your average husband and wife love each other, then grow to tolerate one another's presence – not the settling for a content life most of us subject ourselves to. He loved her more than Jack loved Rose, than Cleopatra loved Mark Antony, than Lancelot loved Guinevere. It was an epic, old-fashioned love that had no bounds and no limits. That monotonous evening you spend staring at a screen with your spouse beside you, counting down the days until death – those were his favourite moments. His arm would rest around her, her head would nestle in the dip beside his shoulder, he'd smell her hair, and he'd think *God, how did I get so lucky.*

Then she'd talk about how she was getting restless and bored. He'd listen to her, wishing she was as happy as he was, just sitting there, doing nothing all evening but doing it together.

To Harry, she was a coup.

To someone like Ben, she was an expectation.

During these long evenings they would spend together, enduring what others suffer as a mundane existence, he would often look at her and wonder – *why?*

Why would someone who could do so, so much better choose to spend their life with someone like him? Especially someone so 'out of his league' – and he put would place the term 'out of his league' in inverted commas, as he believed it to be a ridiculous concept that suggested one's looks determines one's worth in a relationship.

But it wasn't just her looks.

To be in the presence of Lucy was to be riveted by the grace of magnificence. Her conversation was intellectual, her humour naughty, and her sass eloquently playful. When she received a sexist catcall whilst walking down the street, as a beautiful woman like her inevitably does – she could respond with a clever retort that would leave even the most hardened of sexual predators feeling like a fool. She could spark a debate and fuel both sides with passion and articulacy Harry couldn't match. She could produce witty flirtations that made Harry sweat and he couldn't even brave a response.

Harry resented social situations. Every interaction with another person was a blow to the dam of his mental fatigue, and it only took a few cracks for the water to break down its sturdy barrier. He was introverted by nature and dreaded the exhaustion of human contact. He would either say the wrong thing or have nothing to say, and leave the other person wondering who the hell they had just spoken to.

He knew that anyone who met them as a couple would, at some point, whether consciously or unconsciously, consider how mismatched they were. A bizarre coupling. Two people you would not often put together. One of them was the beautiful talk of the party, and the other was the runt who no one wanted to invite in the first place.

Whilst Lucy's time was spent furthering her career and planning dinner dates with friends, Harry spent his time obsessed with his computer games, an obsession that had taken over his life ever since he'd ever set his hands on a Sega Megadrive at seven-years-old.

Once, his ambition had been to become a computer game designer – but, like most endeavours Harry had, he'd realised there was too much competition and, therefore, he would be too unlikely to succeed. Whilst Lucy's drive forced her to excel in everything she did, Harry's despondency meant that he settled for a mundane job as a software programmer in a company no one heard of, sitting at a desk that didn't matter, next to co-workers who would die without anyone remembering them.

In looks, Harry typified the computer nerd stereotype – he was scrawny, with unkempt, messy hair, eyes that stared, and a voice that rarely produced enough volume to be heard.

Lucy was as far from this as one could get.

She was a spritely, young, ball of enthusiastic, social energy. She was petite, with a cute, babyish face, piercing green eyes, and one of those smiles that makes a man question everything. She was five years younger than Harry, meaning he was in his late twenties, and her in her early twenties; which was Harry's explanation as to why their ideal evenings differed so much.

On a Friday night, Harry would play Call of Duty online

while Lucy put on a dress that clung to her body in all the right places, applied her makeup, then drifted to the club where she'd dance the night away. At university Harry had been eager to partake in this; now, however, he'd rather have a cup of tea, a biscuit, and hide his pale face away from the world.

In all honesty, he'd only ever gone on nights out at university because Lucy had coerced him to doing so, and he was relieved they were now at the point he could say *no*.

Despite this huge contradiction in personalities they still fell in love, they still got married, and they still lived happily ever after.

But, in the movies, immediately following the happy ending, are the words *The End.*

The lives of the characters cease, and you leave the cinema satisfied that they are content forever.

In real life, however, *The End* means just that: the end of the happy ever after.

For it is after *The End* when the repetition of life enters a marriage, and that crazy love dies and morphs into subdued despondence.

Lucy was always good enough for Harry. For him, she was the happy ever after, he would never tire of her; but he always worried that this was not reciprocated. He was certain that someone like her would someday end up craving more.

And, unfortunately, he was right.

And it didn't take that long.

Which leads us to the night in question.

The night that began with him stood in the kitchen, staring at nothing, forcing his mind into absence as thought was simply too much to bear.

He took another sip of his beer. He was going to need it.

"Are you sure you want to do this?" Lucy asked as she slid into the room.

Wow, he thought. She looked *killer*. Her black dress glided off her curves like wind down a mountain, highlighting each perfect shape of her body with maximum precision. Her makeup had been subtly applied in a way that highlighted the faultlessness of her facial features, and her body had the delicate aroma of sparsely placed perfume.

He hadn't expected her to get so dressed up for this.

But why wouldn't she?

You'd want to look good for this situation, of course you would.

But this good?

He tried to remember the last time she'd dressed up like this for him.

He stopped himself, as he didn't like where that though led.

"Yeah," he reluctantly answered.

She tucked her arms around his waist.

"Remember how much I love you," she said.

He nodded. Was he meant to say it back?

He didn't feel much like saying it back.

He loved her, absolutely – it just didn't feel right for him to say it to her in that moment.

"And remember, we're being fair, like we spoke about."

Ah, yes. Fairness. Harry remembered this conversation. Out of sheer desperation not to lose her he had agreed to this, and this agreement was shortly followed by a promise that, on a separate occasion, Harry could invite another woman into the bedroom in return. Therefore, both of them would have a session that satisfied them.

Sadly, Harry wasn't as excited at this prospect as she was.

He never told her this, but he had no wish to invite

another woman into the bedroom. She alone was enough. Monogamy had never been something he had to force on himself; it was something he willingly did.

"You know you can back out of this," she reminded him. "But it would probably, kinda, need to be now."

She was telling him he could back out of this. Those were the words he was hearing, and they were great words, yes.

But could he *really*?

It was late now. Ben was almost there.

He just kept telling himself:

This is what makes her happy.

This is what makes her happy.

This is what makes–

He sighed, covering it up as a yawn so Lucy wouldn't see it.

He would do whatever it took to make her content. Anything. This marriage was worth saving, and he would do whatever he could to save it.

Even this.

Even this.

The doorbell rang. Three chimes of doom.

Harry and Lucy shared looks. She looked excited, giddy even. He remembered when she used to look that way at him.

When had they lost that?

She squeezed his hand. A small gesture that meant the world.

That's when he realised; that squeeze wasn't a gesture of reassurance. It was a prompt that he was meant to answer the door.

He took the long walk to the entrance, closing his eyes and willing himself to understand his reasons, understand their reasons, understand *her* reasons. Just to remind himself that he had to do whatever it took.

Whatever it took.

He opened the door.

"Hi," said the chiselled face of a man. He looked how people would expect a person like Lucy's husband should look. "I'm Ben."

2
THEN - HARRY

I FIRST MET LUCY IN THE STUDENT UNION BAR OF OUR university. For her, it was fresher's week. She was eighteen, so eager to meet people, talking to everyone – literally, she talked and hugged and laughed and just had a hell of a time.

I was twenty-three years old, just about to begin my PhD. With my undergraduate and master's degrees done, I was optimistic about the opportunity to become a doctor in programming and what it was going to do for my career. It all seemed so perfect, like it was all finally coming together.

I was reluctantly dragged out by my housemates, who took me to the bar and immediately abandoned me. There was a group of girls and they decided to go talk to them, eager to hit on the new blood.

I was not.

Even in a group, talking to women was not something I'd ever really done. I'd only had one girlfriend, and that was when I was fourteen and it only lasted about three weeks; she dumped me because she said I couldn't kiss properly. I don't really understand what was so wrong about it, I just pursed my lips and put them against hers, but after ten seconds she pulled away and hit me and told me that I need to move my lips or my tongue or whatever – either way, it was not something I was apparently doing correctly. She told everyone, and by the end of the week I was known as the freak who can't kiss.

"Hello," came the keen voice of a beautiful young woman who, for some reason, was talking to me.

"Hi," I said, nervously averting my eyes back to my drink placed perfectly on the bar. I took a sip in attempt to avoid having to say anymore.

"You look lonely, do you want to come sit with us?"

Do I want to go sit with you?

Wow. She was so blunt. I suppose this is what people do in fresher's week as they try to meet new people, but it struck me as incredibly forward and incredibly odd. I wanted to leave, but even at this point she already had a hold on me.

"I'm not – no – I mean thanks, but no."

Stupid me.

I could have made friends. Blossoming relationships could have developed, but I turned it down. Because I was what – *shy*? Not confident enough?

"That's fine, I'll stay here and talk to you then," she persisted, and it made me wonder; why? Why was she persisting? She didn't know me. "What's your name?"

I had no idea what to say. What to tell her.

I mean, my name would have been a good idea, yes – but beyond that, I wanted to be left alone.

Or did I?

Was it just that I felt intimidated by an attractive woman talking to me that meant I wished for solace? That the prospect of conversation with her scared me?

What the hell was wrong with me?

"Harry," I eventually said.

"I'm Lucy. What are you studying, Harry?"

The conversation continued. Somehow, I felt myself sink into it. I turned toward her, engaged with her, and after three hours I knew the names of her entire family, her school background, her hobbies, her interests, her feelings about coming to university, her excitement over her course and her eagerness to meet everyone and *fuck* I was enthralled within minutes. She was incredible, the most interesting person I've ever met, the only person I've met that managed to get me talking, the only person actually willing to see past my blatant social terrors and take the time to really get to know me. She was lovely, and beautiful, so beautiful, not that it's everything, but I just found it remarkable that a woman so beautiful would talk to *me*.

And that was the night I lost my virginity.

3

NOW

He was everything Harry was not – or, at least, everything Harry believed himself not to be.

In fact, Harry wondered why such a man would need to use the internet to find sex at all. With his perfectly symmetrical, rounded facial features, sculpted pectoral muscles, and charming killer smile, he could probably walk into a bar anywhere in the country and instantly be able to talk his way into a woman's bedroom, whether her husband was there or not.

Harry could see Lucy trying to contain her excitement. He knew she was startled by his handsome features, perhaps even a little surprised, but she was at least trying to save Harry's feelings; something he wasn't entirely sure he was grateful for. The whole situation was based on honesty, it was as a result of open conversations and hearts on sleeves and words never left unspoken – and, if she was beginning to hide things to save his feelings, she was doing the complete reverse of what they'd supposedly intended.

Then again, did he actually want her to be honest – or was he just picking the whole shitty situation apart?

Ben didn't even accept a drink.

Within ten minutes they were in the bedroom and they were stripping off and Harry was looking at Ben's body then looking at his own, then looking at Ben's looking at his at Ben's at his at Ben's at his and he just had to remind himself – *this is what I agreed to.*

This was what he was doing to *save his marriage.*

Part of him was aroused by the situation, of course. He had always fantasised about dominating Lucy, which was strange, because he considered his personality to be as far from dominating as he could get. Adding another person to the bedroom that would mean both of them were simultaneously dominating her excited him on some primal level – he just wished that the person he was dominating her with also had the scrawny, flat muscles that pressed against his chest too.

Lucy made sure to kiss both of them.

But what was the point?

Harry's presence was just a kind favour to his ego.

They stood either side of her, taking turns, one kissing her neck as the other kissed her mouth, then vice versa, and Harry couldn't help but think that this meant Ben's saliva was inadvertently being transferred to his mouth. He didn't want to look at Ben, never mind taste him, but he was always there, in a part of him or a part of her.

The entire thing lasted forty-two minutes. Harry knew this because he was irately timing it. The clock had read 9.46p.m. when they started. This was far later than they'd ever had sex. If Harry tried to have sex with her this late, she would say she was too tired; for them to have sex, it would need to be pre-dinner or not at all. As it was, she seemed full of energy and full of enjoyment and she moaned and moaned and moaned; for both of them, never one more than the other, as if deliberately.

They were both involved at all times. If Ben was behind her, penetrating from reverse, pounding her with a masculine grunt upon each thrust, then Lucy ensured that either her hand was grabbing hold of Harry's cock, or that it was in her mouth. Despite this, whilst he was pounding her and her body was continually spasming, she didn't have much concentration to spare on what she was doing to Harry, meaning that his cock was either just held in her hand or left to roam freely about her mouth, like a lonely, idol man hanging around in an empty room. She seemed to forget that he was inside of her too, albeit from the 'less exciting end', but her hands told him she was still alive, her hands that gripped the side of his waist; the harder the grip the harder the orgasm. Ben screamed as she screamed and Harry didn't scream but grabbed her hair and this made her scream more as he moved her dormant head back and forth over his cock because, dammit, Ben and Lucy weren't going to be the only ones having some fucking satisfaction.

Eventually, Lucy turned around and lay on her back, inviting Harry into her. He entered and thrust with all the energy he had, even though he was out of breath in seconds and his thighs ached, he still thrust harder and harder because he did not want to be beaten. He looked into her eyes as he did this and she looked back with that helpless satisfied face she had when she was on the brink of climax and just as she was, Ben's arse appeared next to his face, and Ben's penis entered her mouth. Harry continued on top, continued to thrust, but he had to pull his head out the way as Ben lay out as if he was doing a press up and continually thrusted his cock in and out of her gob, never caring if she was willingly sucking, just thrusting it in and out, in and out, while Harry just tried to keep his face out of the way.

In the end, Ben pulled out of her mouth and grabbed her hair, pulling her off Harry, and made her go to her knees. He rubbed his own cock over her face as she held her mouth open for him.

She held. Her mouth. Open. For him.

She'd told Harry that never in "a million years" would she let him ejaculate on her face, but here Ben was, grabbing her hair to hold her head back and her looking up at him with her lower lip pouting out, ready to take the load.

Harry joined in. If this was the only time he could do it, he'd do it, but he couldn't do it – whatever was happening, nothing was coming out of him.

Ben finished, and she had to blink hard. He was done, and he lay back on the bed, letting his breathing subside.

Now she looked up at Harry and waited. And waited. And waited. It just wasn't coming, he didn't understand why, God he didn't understand why, but he persisted and she waited patiently, so patiently, Ben's cum encrusting her face as she waited, clumping on her cheeks in the way that PVA glue dries on your fingers, like back in primary school when you'd make art and it would stick to your fingers and you would peel it off.

Why the fuck am I thinking about that now, he thought, willing his penis to do something.

She huffed. He knew she didn't mean to, but she huffed, a sigh of frustration, impatience, hesitation, whatever it was. Ben's cum had dripped over her lips and he hated that, and in the end he had to give up.

But she didn't let him.

She grabbed hold of his cock and rubbed it and put it in her mouth and kept going until he finished and she swallowed it and they were done.

It was done.

It was all done.

All three of them lay on the bed and Harry wished that

Ben would go. His part was done now. He needed to go. He was no longer welcome here.

Without a word, Ben stood and made his way into the bathroom. Harry heard the toilet flush and the shower start and he hoped Ben could find some spare towels as he didn't put any out then he realised he didn't actually care. He'd just shared his wife with the guy, it wasn't like it mattered if they shared a towel.

Harry and Lucy lay there silently, naked. Harry staring at the ceiling, Lucy's eyes blissfully closing.

Her hand crept along the bed and found his. Her fingers interlocked with his and she clutched, and she squeezed, and she held his hand tightly, and they stayed like that for the rest of the night.

[POLICE INTERVIEW TRANSCRIPT]

OFFICER Tell me about Lucy.

HARRY (sighs) Lucy was my wife.

OFFICER Was?

HARRY Yes, Lucy was – *is* – my wife. I love her dearly. All of this was for her.

OFFICER If you love her, why let another guy have sex with her?

HARRY It wasn't quite as black and white as that.

OFFICER Well can you explain your reasons?

HARRY Should I have to?

OFFICER Look at it from our point of view. We have a situation – albeit, a strange one – where some irreparable harm has been done. Your wife – Lucy – is... Well, you tell me.

HARRY Tell you what?

OFFICER What did you do to Lucy?

HARRY I told you. *Nothing.*

OFFICER Then how–

HARRY Ben.

OFFICER The guy who fucked your wife?

HARRY Don't say it like that.

OFFICER But it's what happened isn't it?

HARRY Yes, but don't say it like that.

OFFICER Why not?

HARRY Because I don't like it, that's why! I don't even know what I'm doing here, you're not even asking the right questions. Ben – the guy who we had a threesome with – was not who he said he was.

OFFICER And who did he say he was?

HARRY I... He didn't really.

OFFICER So he wasn't who he said he was, but he didn't say he was anyone?

HARRY Please, you just have to help Lucy.

OFFICER I'm trying, Harry. I'm trying. But you've got to see how this looks.

HARRY Do you know what he did to her?

OFFICER What *he* did?

HARRY Yes!

OFFICER I'm starting to wonder if he did anything at all.

HARRY What?

OFFICER Ben, I'm just starting to wonder if he did anything. Who really hurt Lucy?

HARRY I'm telling you the truth.

OFFICER Okay. So, the truth. What happened? What is it that Ben did that you objected to so much?

4

THEN - LUCY

I FIRST FELL IN LOVE WITH HARRY A FEW WEEKS INTO THE relationship.

I'd met Harry that first night, then we saw each other a few times over the following weeks. I hated it when I turned around and it wasn't Harry that my arm draped over. After a month or so I knew that it was Harry that I wanted.

I know, I know, a few weeks – too soon, right?

It wasn't.

I just knew.

Thing is, I knew he wasn't the kind of guy I normally go for, and I'm pretty sure he was aware of that too. My boyfriend at school was as far from Harry as you could get. Sporty, a gym-freak, laddish.

Hey, maybe that's why I dated Harry. My mum always said that, when you date, you always go for someone who is the far extreme from the last person you dated. So, like, if you dated a really smart rocket scientist for a few years, then for the next person you date you'd try to find someone immensely thick and simple.

Maybe that's a bad example, but I get it. And maybe that's what happened with Harry.

Or maybe I just lucked out.

I remember, we were lying in bed together, our bodies sweaty, post-pleasure. And I knew he was nervous, even then, after all the times we'd done it – but Harry was the kind of person who worried that he was not up to standard.

But he could not be more wrong.

There was something about him that made it special. Special unlike any of the other guys.

He hadn't the highest stamina, nor the most fervent vigour of the others I had sex with throughout our relationship – but he had passion. He had love. He was so doted to me, and I could see that any time

That makes it sound like I was *cheating*, doesn't it?

I *wasn't*.

I never had sex with *anyone* but *him*.

Honestly, I didn't. And if you don't believe me, that means you just *don't* understand.

So this one time, like I was saying – I was looking into his eyes, and he was just looking back at me, amazed, as if he had struck gold, as if he couldn't believe his luck.

His hands searched the delicate curves of my exposed body, his eyes would search my eyes, and I could see him, thinking, *wow – how did I get a girl like this?*

And no, I didn't fall in love with him just because this increased my self-esteem. I fell in love with him because of that innocence. That complete lack of awareness of how much of a catch he actually was.

Is.

Because Harry never left. He's not the kind that leaves.

Not like the *others*.

It was just the thought that Harry would feel so strongly about me, about us – it gave me energy, gave me life, gave me something that just made me want to keep talking to him, keep looking at him, keep playing with his hair that he never combed or gelled or waxed, that would just sit there on his head as an untidy clump of knots.

I loved him for that untidy clump of knots.

He could be so much more handsome if he took care of such things, groomed well, shaved better, styled his hair.

Many of the others did.

But I loved *him* because he *didn't* do those things.

Because he was perfect without needing to.

That he didn't act on any pretence, didn't present himself as anything but what he was – an insecure dork.

And he was my dork.

That is, except, when I stopped craving the dork. When I grew bored of the dork.

When I found myself craving more carnal, more rabid, animalistic, rough love.

And more and more, those were the moments I lusted for.

Something I would come to regret.

5
NOW

THE MATING CALLS OF FAMILIAR BIRDS SUNG AROUND THE morning trees. A shaft of light forced itself through narrow line between the curtains, illuminating the carpet with the joyous announcement of morning. The slightly open window did not flutter the curtains with any kind of breeze, instead letting them lie still in the heat of a summer day bursting with sunlight.

Harry's eyes opened gradually, slowly adjusting to the pleasant morning. His sleep was not ended with a sudden jolt or an unpleasant annoyance, but with a happy loll of his head and a smile.

It took him a while to realise that he was laid on his side with Lucy in his arms, and he had to do a double take to ensure this was real. He couldn't remember the last time he'd woken up spooning her. Their sleeping ritual generally consisted of climbing into bed, having a routine hug, then both leaving for their side of the bed for the rest of the night. Their honeymoon was the last time Harry could remember them actually spooning; the last time they had felt so utterly, completely, triumphantly in love that they were compelled to keep skin contact throughout the night. They were in the Caribbean Islands and they were sticky nights, but nights where they'd rather be stuck together.

Since that honeymoon they had been independent sleepers, but this break in the routine was nice. More than nice. It was magical. He felt that rush of love toward her once more. And, as she lay soundly asleep, her eyes fluttering with the beauty of her morning smile, she held onto his arm, holding it across her, making sure that he would not leave this position.

He placed his lips gently on the base of her neck and rested them there for a few seconds. He wouldn't have dared do this a night ago – if he'd have awoken her through an affectionately placed kiss she would have been furious. To her, there was a time and place, and that time and place was not when it compromised her sleep. But, as it was, she responded to this delicate kiss just above her spine with a delectable moan of bliss.

"Hey, you," she said softly, her voice purring. "How did you sleep?"

"Soundly," Harry responded, matching her tone. "Like a baby. Like a log. No, better. Like a baby log."

She giggled at the bad joke.

"Me too," she said. She turned so she was facing him and pushed her body against his. She was still naked and he could feel her breasts against his chest; which prompted a familiar tingle he'd since forgotten.

When was the last time she had slept beside him without pyjamas?

The last time she'd turned around and kissed him without complaining about his morning breath?

The last time she had pressed her bare chest against his as she wrapped her arms around him and he wrapped his arms around hers and they just looked into each other's eyes, truly happy for each other's company?

They sunk into a kiss and it grew passionate. At first, Harry thought this was affection, but once her hand wrapped itself around his erection, he knew it was going to turn into something more.

Within a minute she was atop him, straddling him, riding him. She grinded back and forth, rubbing him, feeling him grow harder and harder. She stretched her body, making her breasts stick prominently into the air, two perfect pyramids parading themselves off her body. He gazed up at her, struck by her sexiness – this was more than just beauty; she exuded sexuality. Raw, powerful, carnal sexual lust poured down her body in sweat as she pleasured him with the vigour of a savage animal, until they both screamed and exploded in a simultaneous orgasm, and she collapsed beside him, again in his arms, again as close as she could get.

Another question he wondered: *when was the last time we had morning sex?*

Their sex life was routine, planned, and set in restrictions. Not too late as you get too tired, not too early as you want to beat that work traffic. But this, for the first time in so long, was exhilarating. Renewed, like everything was fresh, everything was starting again.

"Why don't you go get us a coffee?" she whispered in his ear. "I'll have a shower, then maybe we can get some breakfast and watch some crappy TV shows in bed?"

Oh, God yes. Yes. This was how he'd wished it would be for so long. *So long.*

"Sounds good," he answered, playing it cool. She kissed him on the cheek and practically danced into the bathroom.

Harry went through the wardrobe draws and took out a pair of pyjama trousers. He put them on and caught sight of himself in the mirror. Sweaty, smiling, and dare he say, *rugged.*

With a smile and a hum he bounced his way downstairs. A pile of mail sat on the floor beneath the letter box. They all looked like bills. They could wait.

He made his way into the kitchen.

He stopped dead.

He had assumed this guy had gone. Left as soon as his part had been played.

"Hey, man," said Ben. Sitting at the table, in Harry's dressing gown, eating Harry's cereal, drinking coffee out of Harry's favourite mug.

Why the hell was he still here?

6

THEN - BEN

I FIRST MET HARRY AND LUCY THE WAY THAT MOST PEOPLE meet people nowadays – *online.*

That's my story, anyway.

I can't break my story. It's not allowed. I have to stay completely, unobtrusively, me. Or she won't like it.

The website was threesomefinder.com – and I tell you, there are some interesting freaks on there. My particular favourite was a couple requesting a third party to go dogging with them. This couple was so obese they practically had their own orbit. They wore feathered eye masks, as if that would hide the identity of those fat fucks.

Another more attractive couple requested you dress up like a Shetland pony – not just pony, but a *Shetland* pony, whatever the fuck that was.

There was a couple that only wanted people who were willing to die their hair ginger and curl it, eat marzipan while they came, or just plain get pissed on. Don't get me wrong, I'm always for a bit of watersports, but I draw the line at marzipan.

Fucking weirdos.

But these two, this wonderful couple of Harry and Lucy, presented themselves as normal – normal in a way that no other couple on this website had. And I was intrigued. They couldn't be normal, there is no *normal,* there are only desperate couples with strange sexual fantasies and a willingness to act out the most sordid of scenarios.

So I looked into them.

Facebook, work records, involvement in social activities.

I had to go beyond that.

I had to go the marriage counselling services. I had to look on their records – not tough to get hold of when you know what you're doing – and I looked into the nightmare that was their relationship.

And if, honestly, the only way for this Harry guy to fix the monotony of their marriage was to watch another guy stick his dick deep into his wife's snatch – then hey, who am I to refuse to save their relationship?

I uploaded my photo – one from a few years ago, of course, one before I bought a gym membership. One where I didn't look intimidating to guys like this, one where I didn't look like the last person a guy would want to invite into the bedroom and watch pork his wife. That last person you would ever want to feel threatened by.

After all, my body does look fucking awesome. But I can say that, I can be a little arrogant, because I have worked my perfectly chiselled arse off for it. I have sweated over weights and ab exercises and all of that shit to have this perfect body, to have moulded abs and bursting biceps and pecks that punch through my shirt with such definition it is like I'm a moulded fucking statue. Not to mention my humungous dick that will reach places he couldn't even poke at.

I initiated contact, because that's what Lucy wanted. That's how she wanted my story to be.

I wrote:

. . .

Hey guys, my name is Ben. I'm emailing because I saw your profile on ThreesomeFinder and I wondered if you'd be interested in checking me out. You look like a nice couple, and far more normal than some of the strange pairings I find on here! (I mean, seriously, what's with that?) Please get back in touch if you're interested.

It took twenty minutes for her to reply. Not for *them* to reply – for *her* to reply.

How telling.

Hi Ben, thanks for getting in touch. It's nice to see a profile of probably the only other normal person on this site! I'll need to talk to my husband, but I think we can arrange something. Chat soon.

She didn't even get to know me.

How desperate was this woman for a release from her daily, empty marriage with this sexless sucker she's betrothed to, that she would reply so instantly with an affirmative answer and a strong confirmation?

I mean, who is this guy? What fucking loser could he be?

Probably a dork. Someone who spends more time playing on his computer games than playing with his wife's clit.

Maybe he's never even done that.

Maybe that's why she hates being stuck with him.

God, imagine that.

Being stuck with someone who does nothing for you.

That's where I come in.

My backstory was set. My name was set, my face, my character, it was all exactly as she wanted.

So I told Harry to move aside. He could come back when he wished.

They needed some excitement, I gave it to them.

Oh, boy, did I give it to them.

I replied, and we set a date for two days later.

[POLICE INTERVIEW TRANSCRIPT]

OFFICER Tell me about Ben Davies.

HARRY Pfft. Psychopath. Monster.

OFFICER Could you be a little more specific?

HARRY About what? About how he fucked my wife? About how he tortured her? And me?

OFFICER I thought you said the sex was consensual.

HARRY It was! I…

OFFICER Was it rough sex?

HARRY … What?

OFFICER The consensual sex between your wife and Ben Davies. Was it rough?

HARRY I… Well… isn't sex normally rough? Or, I mean, a little bit, at least? I mean, you don't need to go all dominatrix, but you still have a bit of grabbing and biting.

OFFICER So there was grabbing and biting?

HARRY No! I mean, I – I didn't see any.

OFFICER But there could have been?

HARRY It was a bit of a blur. I don't know if I mentioned this, but he *fucked* and *tortured* my wife.

OFFICER I'm just trying to explain the lacerations and the injuries.

HARRY They were from the torturing.

OFFICER But they could have been from the sex?

HARRY What? No!

OFFICER But you just admitted there may have been a bit of rough play to the sex.

HARRY I said I didn't know. I was a bit anxious, and I didn't really want to watch everything he did.

OFFICER And you? Were you rough with her?

HARRY What?

OFFICER You said it was a threesome.

HARRY Yes, it was.

OFFICER So were you rough with her?

HARRY Are you implying I could have done this?

OFFICER Answer the question.

HARRY No! I – I wasn't any more or less rough than during normal sex, but I certainly didn't torture her.

OFFICER But Ben Davies did?

HARRY Yes!

OFFICER Was there any rough sex between you and Ben Davies?

HARRY What? No! No! I am a heterosexual man, there was no – there was nothing between – we just focussed on her, not on each other. I've already told you this.

OFFICER And after this sex, what happened then?

HARRY We fell asleep.

OFFICER What, you, Lucy and Ben Davies?

HARRY No, I mean me and Lucy, we fell asleep. We assumed Ben had gone.

OFFICER Why did you assume that?

HARRY Because, well, his part was over, there was no – no need for him to – he needn't been there. He'd done what he came for.

OFFICER But you didn't see him leave.

HARRY Why does that matter?

OFFICER I'm just finding some discrepancies between what you said happened and what you saw.

HARRY Ben Davies is a psychopath. He tortured us until we begged. He made us go insane.

OFFICER Yes, but you aren't being particularly specific about what that meant.

HARRY Well then what could I be more specific about?

OFFICER You said he didn't leave that night. When did you discover he hadn't?

HARRY The morning.

OFFICER What happened then?

HARRY I really don't want to… I've already told your colleagues, please don't make me relive it…

OFFICER Harry, we need to know. If you're saying what happened, happened, then we need to–

HARRY Okay, okay. Fine. (*pause*). I'll tell you.

7
NOW

HARRY FOUND HIMSELF CAUGHT IN THE CROSSFIRE BETWEEN attacks of confusion and bombardments of anger.

Why was he still here?

I mean, Harry hadn't paid any attention to whether the guy had left, but the assumption surely was that he wasn't going to stay the night.

Where had he even slept?

He'd walked past the spare room, but he hadn't looked in or taken any notice of whether the bed was unmade or not.

"Hey," Ben said, as if it was Christmas morning and he was greeting his family before presents. "How are you feeling this morning?"

Harry watched with his jaw open as Ben shovelled too much cereal into his mouth and a dribble of milk cascaded down his flawless chin in a few snail trails of thick white.

"Hi," Harry said, and went to question Ben on why he was still there, then didn't.

The questions hung on his lips like a precariously balanced hanger on a faulty hook.

What the hell are you still doing here?

Why haven't you left?

Did you really think you were going to get breakfast after that?

"Have a seat," Ben instructed, pushing out the chair next to him. "Have some breakfast, why don't you?"

The audacity! The sheer audacity! Not only was this man eating Harry's food, this man who only the previous night had fucked his wife – which was a *onetime thing* – he was now inviting Ben to have breakfast in his own house, in his own chair, eating his own cereal.

How did this guy do this?

Harry would never have the balls to take over someone else's house in such a way.

Then again, he'd never have the balls to have sex with someone else's wife in front of them.

There were huge differences between him and Ben, and Ben's forwardness was one of them.

But that was the point, wasn't it?

They were designed to be different.

Ben had the balls for all occasions, and Harry had the balls for…

Hell, he wouldn't have the balls for anything. If a man barged into him in a busy street, it would be Harry that apologised.

"Well? You having breakfast, or what?"

Harry reluctantly took the chair that had been pushed out for him, cautiously seating himself as if he were sitting above a bomb, or next to a crocodile. He never took his disdainful look of confusion off Ben for a second.

"Let's see what we got here," Ben said, rummaging through the boxes of cereal in front of him that would normally belong in the cupboard but had been taken out and strewn across the surface. "We got Frosties. Rice Crispies. Some honey fruit shit."

"I know," Harry reluctantly said, willing himself to have a backbone. "They're my cereals."

"Right," Ben acknowledged, shaking his head stupidly. "Of course."

Ben took another large mouthful of cereal, splashing most of it back into his bowl, the splashes of which bounced upon the surface in puddles.

"Harry, where are you!" Lucy's voice sung and she appeared in the doorway, happy, content, and wearing nothing but a towel wrapped around her head. As soon as she saw Ben, she halted, quickly snatched the towel from around her head and fastened it around her body.

"Don't worry," Ben said smugly, "I've already seen it."

"Why is Ben still here?" Lucy asked, poised in the doorway, giving a *what-the-fuck* expression to Harry, who appeared sat casually next to him.

"What do you mean?" Ben asked, shovelling the final spoonfuls into his mouth.

"I thought you'd have left last night. I mean, afterwards. The agreement was that I'd return to Harry. I mean - *just Harry.*"

Ben shrugged. "I figured you guys would like some breakfast. I could do you some eggs or something if you'd prefer."

"I'm fine, thank you," Lucy answered, shooting a look at Ben. "We'll make our own breakfast, honestly, I think it's best if you just made your way home," she insisted as pleasantly and politely as she could make herself sound amongst the confusion.

Ben didn't look at her. He kept his face blank, stuck between thoughts. He took his dish and walked over to the sink where he washed it up.

"We'll see to that," Lucy said. "Honestly, I think it's probably best if you go."

Ben grinned. A lecherous snake-like grin.

"Didn't say that a minute ago," Ben said. "A minute ago, Harry was happy for me to stay, ready to have breakfast with me."

"No, I–" Harry shot Lucy a look, a look that told her not to believe it. "No, I was just shocked, that you were still here, of course. I do think – I think you should go."

"So it takes her," Ben pointed at Lucy, "to get you," he pointed at Harry, "to grow a pair and tell me to leave."

"I–" Harry wasn't sure what to say.

"I see. So if you want something done, you got to get the woman to do it."

"I am not *the woman,*" Lucy defied. "And, honestly, I think you're being a little rude now."

Ben snorted a high-pitched guffaw. "Rude?"

"Yes, rude."

"Was it rude when I was in your snatch last night?"

"Okay!" Harry said, his hands on his hips.

Ben waited.

"Okay what?" Ben laughed. "Isn't that when you're supposed to charge up to me and defend your woman?"

"I do not *need* him to defend me," Lucy interrupted, wrapping her arms around the top of her chest where her skin was still exposed, feeling more and more naked as the conversation went on. "And, honestly, it is time you leave."

Ben held his gaze on her. Looked her up and down, making her feel even more disgusting.

"Fine," said Ben. "I'll call a taxi."

He withdrew his phone and held it to his ear.

As he waited for it to ring, his eyes turned back to Lucy. They went down to her exposed legs, still with droplets of water running down her thighs, then back to the skin below her shoulders. Beneath that towel was her breasts, those breasts he had grabbed on last night, and she knew it, and he knew she knew it, and he knew that she knew that this was in his mind; his smile told her everything.

"Hello, can I book a taxi please? … Yes, 60 Shoreditch Avenue… That would be lovely."

He hung up the phone.

Silence gathered between them like a million elephants in a room.

"It will be twenty minutes," Ben finally said, his eyes still scanning her, never stopping for a break.

8
NOW

Twenty long minutes went by with Harry huddled close to Lucy, his arm around her, both of them staring longingly out of the living room window. In every car that went by they searched for stickers that would indicate a taxi, for something atop the roof, for anything that would give them some sense of release from the excruciating tension they were suffering silently together.

They could hear him, sitting in the kitchen, occasionally shuffling. Shifting his body. Doing nothing.

Twenty minutes turned into thirty, which turned into forty, and Harry could feel himself shaking. He tried to hide it from Lucy, but he knew she could feel it too, his quivering arms, his seizing chest. The pit of his stomach rose up through his lungs, searching his insides like the wild snakes of Madusa's hair, hissing and snapping.

"The taxi's not coming," Lucy decided.

"Come on, we don't know that," Harry insisted, more to himself than to Lucy.

"Harry, come off it. How long have we been waiting here?"

Harry glanced at his watch, even though he knew the answer.

"It could be running late."

Lucy turned toward him and sighed, sinking into his embrace, something that gave Harry a brief flicker of respite, and he was glad that she was there and he wasn't dealing with this guy alone; even if the relief was abruptly destroyed by the sound of fingers drumming the kitchen table.

"What are we going to do?" Harry asked.

"I told you that Ben would have to go, Harry."

"What?"

"Make him go. It's up to you."

"It's not up to me – how am I supposed to?"

"He's your… *Thing.*"

"What do you mean, my *thing*?" He looked over his shoulder and peered into the kitchen, then back to Lucy.

She struggled to explain what she meant.

Somehow, she thought he'd just understand.

"Maybe we should just call the police," he concluded.

"And tell them what?"

Lucy shook her head. This was ridiculous.

"I'm going to go get dressed," Lucy decided, her wet hair having dried in rabid curls. "Make him go. Ask him where his taxi is if that helps you to believe it. I'll get my phone in case we need to call the police – and I really don't want to have to do that, because that would be stupid."

Lucy marched up the stairs, leaving Harry alone to turn and face the door. Somehow, his legs didn't carry him into the kitchen as he instructed them to. Instead, they spread through the ground like roots of a tree, sinking through soil and fixing him in place.

He willed his feet upwards, and he pulled them out of those roots, wrenching them from the floor, and feebly tiptoed into the kitchen.

There he was. Ben. Sat nonchalantly on the chair, one arm draped over the back of it, another resting on the table on which he tapped his fingers with faint precision.

"Is the taxi going to be here soon?" Harry asked, his voice breaking.

Ben snorted a laugh, and that was all the answer Harry received.

"Is it?" Harry tried again, trying to sound forceful despite his voice coming out in nothing but a quiver.

"Sit down," Ben said, his voice slow and casual, like he was talking to a friend in the pub about how to rob a bank. "Chill out, relax with me, come on."

"I don't want to sit down."

Ben snorted again. This infuriated Harry, but he said nothing. Instead, he consciously fixed his body language, spreading his feet shoulder width apart, folding his arms, and deadening his expression. This only prompted another snort.

"Jesus, man," Ben continued. "You are a joke."

"What?"

"Look at you, trying to act all hard, trying to be the big man. If you were the big man in the first place, you wouldn't even be in this situation."

"What situation?"

Ben grinned that same grin and snorted that same snort. He threw his iPhone on the table. The screen was blank.

Harry strode forward and picked up the iPhone, pushing the home button, the on button – nothing happening.

"It's out of battery, mate. It's been out of battery since I got here."

Harry looked over his shoulder. Wished Lucy would appear. Appear with her phone, having called the police, having done something to help.

Ben stood. He sauntered toward Harry.

Harry backed away.

Then he decided he shouldn't have to back away, it's his house.

Ben grinned. Harry still backed away.

Lucy appeared in the doorway.

"Where's my phone?" she demanded.

"Lucy," Harry quickly spoke, "he hasn't called a taxi, there isn't one coming, his phone's not even on."

"Where is *my* phone?" Lucy said with conviction, ignoring Harry's weeping.

Ben waited, then coolly shrugged his shoulders.

Lucy charged forward, showing the aggression Harry wished he'd shown.

"What have you done with my phone?"

Ben shrugged again. "I don't know where your phone is."

Lucy looked to Harry. "Harry? Where is my phone."

No response.

"We're leaving," she told him.

Harry looked back at Ben. "You hear that? Leave now, or we'll call the police."

"And tell them what? You asked a guy to fuck your wife, and then he didn't call a taxi?"

Lucy held onto Harry's hand and tugged, pulling him away.

"Please, just leave," Harry said. "Just go, and we'll forget all about this."

Ben grinned.

That fucking grin.

"Come on, Harry, if this is what we have to do," she insisted, and Harry gave in, allowing himself to be dragged away.

Harry wasn't entirely sure what happened next.

He had placed his hand on the door handle, overcome with a huge wave of relief that they were leaving this situation and they were leaving it together.

Together. Finally.

But Harry's wrist hadn't even turned the handle before the door shook in a vigorous slam.

He looked to his side and saw Lucy's groggy eyes looking back at his, a dribble of blood making the journey from her nose to her chin.

A tight fist grabbed the back of her hair and shoved her face into the door once more.

Her body discarded itself into a messy lump on the stained carpet, leaving a bloody imprint against the pile of bills.

Ben reached in front of Harry, took the key to the front door in his hand, turned it slowly, so slowly, looking into Harry's eyes the entire time; then took out the key and placed it in his pocket.

"Get on your fucking knees," Ben said, his voice so slow, so low-pitched.

Harry did as he was told.

9

THEN - HARRY

I THINK SHE LIKED THAT I WAS A VIRGIN WHEN SHE MET ME.

I certainly didn't like that she was not, nor that her sexual experience was vastly superior to mine. I mean, I never knew what her 'number' was – but that's because I never wanted to ask. It would mean that I'd endure every minute we spent making love under a hypnotic feeling of inferiority.

But for her, she gained pleasure from having nothing to be jealous about. She found excitement in being a *teacher*.

I never found this patronising, which I probably should have done – after all, who wants their girlfriend constantly pointing out their sexual errors?

But I enjoyed the gratitude she derived from showing me what I needed to do – what I could caress or lick or penetrate to give her more pleasure. It was like, however much I disliked that she had so much more experience than me, it served a purpose. It had directed her to me, where she could guide me to becoming the best she ever had.

For the first few months we barely left the bedroom. There were days we'd wake up in her halls of residence room, have sex, then decide to go into town, then as we walk into town, go past my halls of residence room and decide to use it to have sex again.

Some of those days I counted four times. *Four times a day*, that is.

The thought is crazy. I don't think Lucy could bear four times a month now.

Those early days especially, I remember her smile, how she'd have this cheeky glint in her eyes as she placed both hands atop my head, guiding me downwards. I would get there, face-to-face with her genitalia, look at them, and feel like there was a whole sitcom audience watching me, ready to laugh at how clueless I was.

It didn't matter. She'd grab my hair and she'd move my head, side to side, up and down. I'd bat my tongue like I was slurping up water and she'd put me in the position she'd want and she'd moan, she'd scream, she'd cry out my name – and I *loved* it when she cried out my name.

If she's crying out *my* name, it means I'm the one she's thinking of.

And how many of us actually fantasise about our partner?

As her head lolled back and her eyes closed she could picture anything she wanted. She would have the choice of any scenario projected onto the cinema screen of her mind and I wouldn't know – but, if she was shouting my name, I'd know it was *me* on that screen, and me alone.

There was one time at university that a formal complaint was lodged against us. She'd received a letter tucked under her door that read:

Dear Miss Lucy Hess,

. . .

We have received numerous complaints about noises coming from of your room that disrupt other's sleep.

Can I please remind you that we have a policy of no noise after 11p.m.

Should these complaints persist we will investigate further.

Kind Regards,
Accommodation Officer

We laughed as if it was the most absurd, preposterous, ridiculous thing ever. A waste of time for whoever wrote it.

We had sex right on top of that letter because we thought it would be hilarious. We used it to wipe down the bed afterwards, then considered getting it framed – which we would have done if it had still been readable after we'd finished with it.

It seemed like it was marriage that killed it.

Two weeks after our honeymoon and she didn't give a shit anymore.

I flicked my tongue so quickly it grew stiff. I sped up until my jaw locked and ached and I rode through the pain just to make her happy, but she didn't even react.

"Lucy?" I asked. "Lucy, is this all right?"

"Mm," was her response.

I looked up. Her eyes were closed. Her head lolled to the side.

Her eyes were always closed during sex – throughout the *whole* of sex, so this was nothing new.

I mean, once upon a time they weren't closed, but it was a common occurrence now.

But, if I hadn't known that her closing her eyes and laying limp for the entire experience was normal, I would have assumed that she was asleep.

"Lucy?" I prompted.

I went down again, watching her, and her body didn't convulse or respond, her mouth didn't moan or groan, her entire body remained empty. It wasn't even as if she found it unpleasant, or that she wished to tell me what she wanted.

It was as if she was done pretending to care.

"Lucy?" I said.

She didn't even respond this time.

"Lucy?"

I felt sick.

"Lucy?"

That's when I knew Harry's time was about done.

10
NOW

"Lucy?"

Harry felt sick.

"Lucy? Lucy?"

Her body was wrapped in rope like a bow around a gift. Her ankles, her chest, her wrists. Duct tape wrapped around her head so it covered her mouth enough times to keep her quiet.

Still, she didn't wake up.

"Lucy?" Harry pleaded.

He looked up at Ben.

"Put your hands behind your back," he said, grinning wildly at Harry, looking down at him.

Harry hated his life. Not just this situation, but his entire life – in that moment, he wished he'd lived everything differently. Had been a different person.

Harry wished that *Harry* wasn't ever a part of Lucy's life.

He looked up into the eyes of the man who fucked his wife then tied them up and wondered if it would even make a difference if Ben killed him.

Lucy stirred.

Her eyes opened.

"Put your fucking hands behind your fucking back."

Harry obeyed.

[POLICE INTERVIEW TRANSCRIPT]

OFFICER Tell me more about what Ben Davies did to your wife.

(Silence)

OFFICER I know this is tough, Harry, and we don't want to make you keep reliving it, but it's important.

HARRY Can't you just look at the previous statement I made?

OFFICER I have, but I just wish to find out a little more myself.

HARRY Why?

OFFICER Because, like I said, there are a few discrepancies.

HARRY What discrepancies?

OFFICER Between what you're telling me and what forensic analysis is telling me.

HARRY Like what?

OFFICER Like, for example – the marks on your palm fit with the rope used to tie Lucy up.

HARRY That's because he made me do it!

OFFICER He made you tie her up?

HARRY Yes!

OFFICER So talk me through it – who had the rope? You or him?

HARRY I don't know, he – he just seemed to have it.

OFFICER Where did he get it from?

HARRY Probably the basement, if he didn't bring it himself. We have some rope in the basement.

OFFICER How would Ben Davies have known to get rope from the basement?

HARRY How the hell would I know!

OFFICER Right. Okay. So talk me through what happens next. He gives you the rope…

HARRY He tells me to tie Lucy up.

OFFICER To which you say?

HARRY Nothing. I said nothing.

OFFICER Nothing?

HARRY What do you want from me? I said nothing. I just did as I was told.

OFFICER Why?

HARRY I – I don't know.

OFFICER There must be a reason.

HARRY Because I was scared, I guess.

OFFICER Scared of what?

HARRY Scared of what would happen if I didn't do it. To me and Lucy.

OFFICER So you tied her up…

HARRY Yes.

OFFICER Then what?

HARRY Then – then I… I put my hands behind my back to let him tie them there.

OFFICER But again, Harry, that makes no sense.

HARRY Why?

OFFICER Lucy's wrists are covered in rope burns. Yours aren't.

HARRY That's because I didn't do it.

OFFICER You didn't tie your hands?

HARRY I tried. But I wasn't able to.

OFFICER Then what?

HARRY Then – then he made me do things.

OFFICER What things?

(Silence)

OFFICER What things, Harry?

(Silence)

OFFICER Harry, what things?

(Silence)

OFFICER Harry, come on. The problem is I have a dead woman you tell me you loved, and nothing to go on. Tell me the truth.

(Silence)

OFFICER Tell me how Lucy died.

11
NOW

THE WAY BEN SAT ON THE ARMCHAIR INCENSED HARRY'S feeble temperament further. But you know Harry's character well enough by now to know that the boring, drab, pushover would do nothing about it.

"Fine," Ben said. "If you can't tie yourself up, then you're just going to have to do my part for me."

"What?" Harry gasped, soaking the back of his hand with a slither of sweat from his forehead.

Ben's right leg lay over the arm of the chair, swinging like thread dangling over a cat. His left arm draped loosely over the back of the chair, and his right hand rested on his bollocks that snuggled lightly between his wide-open legs.

"Pick her up."

Harry went to put his arms beneath Lucy's armpits.

"No – by her hair."

"Her hair?"

Harry looked down at Lucy, who stared up at him with eyes big and scared and tear ducts flowing. She frantically shook her head, her desperate speech muffled by the duct tape around her mouth.

Harry could just about make out a few words.

"Mmmm... please... stop... mmmmm... gone... too... far... now... mmmm..."

Harry just looked back with his helpless shoulders shrugging and his pained expression wavering. He didn't want to do this, he didn't want to mistreat her, but what could he do – Ben was better than him in every way. Athletically, mentally, sexually. The strength was overpowering and, even if Harry and Lucy's lives weren't being threatened, he was still likely to have obeyed such an intimidating persona.

"I'm so sorry," Harry wept.

His fist wrapped around a large clump of her hair – not just one or two strands, no; he swept her hair upwards with his open palm and grasped his hands around as much hair as he could. He did all he could to screen his mind from her muffled yelps of agony as he helped her up, her knees scraping the carpet, a continual moan as he held her there.

"Now punch her in the gut."

"What!"

"I said punch her in the gut."

"I can't, I can't – I can't do that."

Ben stood, withdrawing a kitchen knife he'd kept hidden. It still had flakes of butter on it.

"Do it or I stab her with her own kitchen knife, then I stab you with her own kitchen knife."

Harry turned to Lucy, wading pathetically from side to side, staring up at Harry. Her expression was a morphed contortion of pain and anger and disbelief that the whole situation had gone this far.

"I'm so sorry," Harry told her.

He retracted his arm far enough back for him to get a large swing, then swung it through her gut with enough force to completely wind her. She wheezed as Harry dropped her, allowing her to squirm on the floor like a worm missing half its body.

Harry stood over her, awkwardly assured, helplessly numb.

Eventually, her breathing returned to normal and, although she was unable to breathe through her mouth, you could still see the movement of the tight duct tape from the rapidity of her outward coughs.

"Excellent," Ben stated.

Harry looked at what he'd done. The mess, the terror, the feeble whimpers of a wife desperately pleading with her husband; her left eye blinking against a clump of blood mixed with tears.

"Now stab her."

A surge of locusts swarmed into his mind from every point – through his ears, through his nose, through his mouth, even through his eyeballs. They swarmed around, beating each other, bombarding the prison of his skull, battering the synapses of his mind. Each locust brought another thought, another surge of denial, or anger, or hostility, or reprieve, or terror. Each locust growing in size, battling the others for prominence.

"What?" he quivered.

Ben said nothing.

Harry looked down and the knife was somehow in his hand.

He could lunge at Ben, stabbing and thrusting and dragging and twisting and doing everything he could to end this bastard's life, to destroy the man who was everything Harry wasn't.

But he didn't. He couldn't.

You might ask why.

Well, so did Harry.

He wanted to know why he didn't kill Ben. Why he

obeyed this man with such demented servitude, doing all the actions that were instructed of him with the obedience of a pathetic dog; salivating for Ben, panting for Ben, playing for Ben, *go fetch, Harry, go fetch – do as you're told. Be a good boy.*

He lifted the knife.

Looked to Ben.

Pictured slitting Ben's throat. Dragging the knife smoothly across the outline of his Adam's apple, spraying the floor like a shaken can of coke.

But it was as if, by killing Ben, he'd be killing a part of himself too.

He couldn't do it.

"Which part of her do you want me to stab?" he asked.

"Dealer's choice," Ben answered.

Harry mounted Lucy. She struggled and he used his spare hand to hold her still, gripping her by the throat, ignoring her eyes, don't look into those eyes, not the eyes, those eyes lie, don't lie, don't look at the eyes.

He plunged the knife into her ribs, held it there, then pulled on it, but it was stuck, as if it was held by chewing gum. He released the knife and she moaned, cried, squirmed.

Harry wasn't moved.

Ben found it hilarious.

"Good," Ben said. "Now kill her."

[POLICE INTERVIEW TRANSCRIPT]

OFFICER I'm not buying it, Harry.

HARRY What? What are you not buying?

OFFICER You had the knife in your hand and you, what – chose not to go at Ben with it, and willingly used it on your wife? Why would you do that?

HARRY I don't know.

OFFICER I'm going to need better than that.

HARRY I don't know!

OFFICER Let me tell you what we found.

HARRY What?

OFFICER We found traces of semen.

HARRY Well, yes you would.

OFFICER And you're telling me Ben Davies ejaculated, what – on her face?

HARRY Yes.

OFFICER And in her hair?

HARRY Yes.

(Silence)

OFFICER We found traces of semen in her hair, Harry.

HARRY Well, yes you would!

OFFICERBut those traces were *your* semen.

(Silence)

HARRY What?

OFFICER There were no traces of semen that wasn't yours, neither internally or externally. Everything we found belonged to you.

HARRY Then test again. That's not possible.

OFFICER In fact, there is no record of Ben Davies' online profile either.

HARRY How? What? I saw it! I saw the profile!

OFFICER We looked at all the deleted profiles, every existing profile matching the name. Nothing.

HARRY I – I don't understand.

OFFICER We even proceeded to search for his laptop to look on that, but his home didn't exist.

HARRY What – how – how is that possible?

OFFICER In fact, Harry, there is no trace of Ben Davies ever having existed at all.

(Silence)

OFFICER Not online, not in person, nothing.

HARRY You're wrong.

OFFICER Harry –

HARRY Are you calling me a liar?

OFFICER Harry, we went beyond just semen. We looked for traces of pubic hair, traces of DNA, finger prints on the objects you've said Ben Davies handled. There is nothing.

HARRY Nothing?

OFFICER Just yours. All yours. Your hair, your DNA, and your finger prints on the objects you said he'd held.

HARRY How? How could that be?

OFFICER You tell me.

HARRY What?

OFFICER It's time to tell the truth, Harry.

HARRY I am!

OFFICER No, you are not. It's time to be honest.

(Silence)

OFFICER What really happened that night, Harry? What really happened?

12
LUCY

OH, GOD, I LOVED IT. IT WAS PROBABLY WHAT BROUGHT US together.

I mean, I know that a relationship shouldn't be based solely on your sex life – and it wasn't – but it was so great to find someone who actually loved the same things as me. Because when you have a quirk, or a special fetish, or something, it's often difficult.

I mean, not that *roleplay* is a particular quirk or fetish that repels people, as such. I mean, it's not autoerotic asphyxiation, or donkey punching, or anything. I'm not asking him to wear a gimp mask while I tug on his testacies in a leather one-piece.

It's just roleplay.

The idea that for one night, or however long it lasts, you get to be who you want to be, and they get to be who you've always wanted them to be. Whatever scenario or fantasy or niche, you become those characters in that moment with that scenario, with that fantasy serving that niche.

And my husband was open to them. God, he was so open. I mean, he'd slept with enough women that he knew what he wanted. He had a body that every woman craved, a personality that made other men hide behind their defence mechanisms. He could have any woman he wanted.

And he chose me.

And that never lost its excitement. It never got dull. Because we were never the same people from one night to the next.

But, after a while, being with someone perfect can get boring. That's why I asked him to roleplay as a character I invented for him.

A character called Harry.

We first used Harry during fresher's week, pretending that I had just started uni and that my husband had been there a few years. He went up to the bar and pretended that we didn't know each other. For once, we pretended that that I was the one with the great amount of sexual experience, and that he was the timid virgin. Like he was some computer-game-obsessed nerd studying for a PhD – don't get me wrong, I admire anyone who commits themselves to such an endeavour, but my husband got by on his looks, not his intelligence.

Unlike Harry.

Although I knew it was rubbish, that he could never just be some scraggly nerdy guy too shy to talk to me, I loved it. Because he got *so* into it. He was like a method actor, changing his clothes and his appearance and his mannerisms – as a result, his performance as Harry was fucking perfect. Honestly, if he ever wanted to be an actor, he'd storm it – but I'm glad he didn't. This way, it's just me that gets this side of him.

So the creation of Ben Davies was easy.

Because that's who he is.

My husband *is* Ben Davies.

We just had to emphasise those particular aspects of himself we wanted for the character of Ben.

So for this night, he would be Harry. He would pretend that Ben was the visitor, that Harry was the man I'd been married to. We pretended that our marriage was boring as shit because that's what it would be like to be married to the character of Harry. That same old person we see so many men become. The shy, good-for-nothing loser who can't please his wife.

Meaning Ben could be the outsider.

And God, he was good at it. He could go between the two so quickly, so effortlessly. He could change his mannerisms and his voice like he was these two completely different people, so much so it really was like I was being fucked by both of them.

When we came up with the fantasy, I knew he'd get into it. That he'd find the role and do it well.

But I never thought he'd actually do it this well.

I mean, I know Harry and Ben back-to-back. I knew both of them so well because I'd slept with both of them so many times. And who he'd wake up as in the morning would depend on how much he'd invested in the role play.

We had other characters too.

Once, he was as a soldier who'd come home for just a week, and he stayed as that soldier for the entire week. It was some of the best sex we ever had. It was all so urgent, so desperate, so keen. Like his life depended on it – because to him, it did depend on it. Because he wasn't Ben anymore. He *was* this soldier.

So, in this fantasy he'd be Harry, and we exaggerated Ben, gave him a slightly crazy edge. That timid character he'd created versus that scary, hidden part of himself.

He'd fuck me as both of them.

Then, as Ben, he'd pretend not to go.

As Harry, he'd get scared with me about it.

He'd pretend to tie me up.

Pretend to tie me up.

Again, the plan was that he'd *pretend* to tie me up.

That's when things changed. When I wanted it to stop.

But it had gone too far by then.

I didn't realise until too late that the person running the shots really, truly, was no longer my husband.

That was when it was meant to stop.

That was when we'd agreed it would stop.

But, you know my husband – when he takes on a role, he takes it on.

It was hot. It was rough. It was everything I wanted. An expert fantasy that brought us together. A perfectly constructed set of characters.

That is, until I felt something hard and hot cushion beneath my ribs. Until I felt something dribbling down my skin like a pool of hot acid. When something sunk into me and released my insides with chronic perfection, to the point that the fantasy was no longer a fantasy, but a reality.

And I wasn't sure if it would ever end.

13

NOW

HARRY SHOOK THE BLOOD OUT OF HIS HAIR.

He willed himself to stop.

Ben told him to keep going.

"But I can't."

"But you must."

"Why?"

"I told you to."

"Please just let me go."

"I told you to kill her."

She looked like a baby. Like a helpless child. Like a morsel missing its mother, a cat being taunted, a dog knowing they are about to be put down.

It was time to put her down.

Harry lifted the knife.

Ben told him he was doing well.

Harry looked into her eyes and told her he was sorry.

"I'm sorry," he whispered.

Ben told him to get over himself.

Harry shook his head. He couldn't do it.

Ben could do it. Ben would do it. He took hold of Harry's wrists and whispered smoothly in his ear.

"Here," Ben said, "We'll do it together."

Feeling Ben's coarse fingers wrapping around his fists, he felt a welcome relief, a sense that he was no longer alone in this, that he had the support he needed.

Ben pressed his body against Harry's back, morphing like they were one, a single unity with double strength carrying out a solitary act of power.

With the comfort of Ben's hands Harry took the gentle nudge and obeyed what he had been told. The silver steel of the knife soared through the air, flickering stains of blood in its wake. It landed in her chest and retracted almost as quickly.

It landed in her throat and he pulled it out with all his strength.

The knife stuck in the muscle of her thigh, wedged neatly inside, and he grabbed it and pulled it out.

Then he stuck it back in again.

In her face.

Her eyes.

Her face once more.

Her breast.

Arm.

Belly.

Lung.

Muscle.

Heart.

Ear. Breast. Thigh.

Face thigh breast ear mouth genitals gut knee throat.

And that was where he left it.

He pushed himself across the room, scampering away, pressing himself against the loose wallpaper that papercut the back of his neck.

Harry didn't notice Ben leave, but he knew that he had.

Harry just stared. Gawped at what he'd done.

Oh dear God.

Realisation awakened him from a trance he'd been stuck in.

She's dead...

He could no longer tell if she was bleeding. She was in an ocean of it. There was more of it than there was of her.

All he could perceive was that she was motionless. Her chest didn't rise and her fingers didn't flicker.

She was dead.

He'd killed her.

Ben had killed her.

14
THEN - HARRY / BEN

SHE SQUEEZED MY HAND. A SMALL GESTURE THAT MEANT THE world.

I knew that meant it was time to change.

My performance as Harry was to pause, albeit very briefly – for the entry of Ben.

I made the doorbell ring. Three chimes of doom. I pretended to answer it, pretended to say hi.

Then I stopped pretending.

See, the best thing about our role play, is that there is no pretending. There's no, "I'm going to play being this character for a bit" – it's "I *am* this character for a bit, and I *will not* change from this character, whatever happens."

Whatever happens.

Lucy says the terrific thing about my roleplaying is the ability to go seamlessly between two characters in the same room. She loved it when I was fucking her as Harry one moment, then fucking her as Ben the other. I'd be all tender and worried and inexperienced and *oh I'm so sad to see this scary man being rough with my delicate wife.*

Then I'd shove Harry away and Ben would take over, *get*

out the way you fucking coward and let me show you how you really should fuck your wife.

Then we finished, and we fell asleep in each other's arms. We fell asleep as Harry and Lucy.

But I'm not Harry. I'm Ben.

Harry is a made-up character. So why was she he sleeping in his arms?

I didn't like it. And that's why I refused to go.

Lucy tried to make it end. But it was too late. I'd assumed my roles with such vigour that neither of them left. But that's why she liked it – because of the roles that I take, and my commitment to them.

I could see in her face that she wasn't liking it anymore. Somewhere in her eyes there was this faraway look, a look of regret.

But I didn't acknowledge it.

I didn't, because neither Harry or Ben would acknowledge it.

I knew their backstory. I knew how Ben found them, how Harry introduced himself as the timid virgin in fresher's week. As if it hadn't been planned beforehand. As if it wasn't all part of the elaborate performance we construct to escape the monotony of our lives.

She suggested one of us takes a taxi.

She didn't want to go on with the roleplay any longer. She wanted it to end, but she didn't want the performance to be destroyed. By making one us leave it meant that there was no breaking character and no breaking the illusion. It just meant that one of us was left and she was back to being with her husband.

But we didn't want to leave.

The plan was not for anyone to leave.

And I had no idea what Ben had instore for Harry.

And I had no idea how much of a gutless piece of shit

Harry was going to be.

But that's the way it goes.

We had an agreement – whatever happens, you *do not* break character.

Whatever happens.

15
NOW - LUCY

I WAS PRACTICALLY DEAD FROM THE MOMENT HE SUNK THE knife into my ribs. I felt it scrape along the surface of my heart, felt its throbbing beat decline.

The world turned to a blur of colours, like a head rush, but quicker.

I watched the man above me that I love, love more than life itself, love more than I ever thought possible – and I saw him lift the knife high above his head and cry. Then I saw the tears go. I saw his face toughen, like he meant it, like this was something he had to do, like I was an object and he was destroying it.

That was Ben right there. Not Harry.

That was Ben.

Not my husband, Ben – but the Ben we had created.

I tried to plead to him to stop. Tried to tell him it was over, the role play was over, it was time to break character, to go back to Ben – not timid, pathetic Harry, not macho, psychotic Ben, but my husband. The kind husband. The husband I…

Too late.

I stopped trying to shout through the layers of duct tape as I felt the knife enter inside of me for the second time.

It didn't feel as I expected it to feel. It was just uncomfortable. It was hot, like the knife had been taken out of the oven, and really tight, like my skin was suddenly opened then pulled together.

The warmth sunk down my skin and I watched as he hit me again.

The only true bit of pain I had was just before I died.

Now *that* was pain. It was scorching, wrenching, twisting, convulsing, entwining, contorting agony. A sudden burst of sun except I felt nothing but the flames. I think I screamed, I don't know, I'm not sure, I'd been trying to scream for ages, but it wasn't like anything could get beyond that duct tape – he'd wrapped it around my mouth so many times. I was already struggling to breathe.

And then I stopped struggling.

I stopped hurting.

After that momentary clinch of pain, it stopped.

And I stopped.

And I no longer existed.

I didn't go to heaven or hell, because there is no such thing. I didn't get reincarnated, because I wasn't so lucky. I didn't even have the chance to come back as a spirit.

I ceased.

Ended.

And that's how I remained.

And that's how I am now.

POLICE INTERVIEW TRANSCRIPT

OFFICER Are we done with this pretence now, Harry?

BEN Harry?

OFFICER Or has Harry left?

BEN Harry… was never here…

OFFICER Do you have anything else to say, Harry?

(Silence)

OFFICER You are under arrest on suspicion of murder, do you understand?

(Silence)

OFFICER You do not have to say anything but it may harm your defence if you do not answer when questioned something that you may later rely on in court. Anything you do say can be given as evidence.

BEN No… No… No…

OFFICER Harry, do you understand?

BEN My name is Ben, not Harry.

OFFICER *(sighs)* I see. And did you murder your wife, Ben?

BEN *(long pause)* … we did it together.

[End of transcript]

16

NOW - BEN

I WATCH.

From outside the window, I just watch.

Harry sitting there, back against the wall, looking at what we've done.

Looking at the corpse we'd created.

My favourite song comes to mind. Big Yellow Taxi by Jodi Mitchell.

Don't it always seem to go that you don't know what you got til it's gone?

Maybe this way, Harry will be grateful for her.

Maybe this way, Harry will realise what he has. He won't invite some jackass in for a threesome; he will work on things, work on their relationship, making it better with them.

Just. Them.

He takes her in his arms. He shakes her. Tries to revive her. She doesn't respond, but of course she wouldn't. We'd done a pretty good job on her.

He rushes to the phone. He dials 999. He tells them they

had an intruder, that the intruder has killed his wife. They ambulance says it's on its way, the police say they are on their way, and it isn't long until I hear the sirens.

I don't bother moving. Or hiding. It's not like they'll see me.

You can't see something that doesn't exist.

So I watch as the paramedics come in but she's announced dead instantly. What could they do? She was a bloody mess.

Harry is uncontrollable. Inconsolable. They have to hold him back, tuck their arms around him, stop him from thrashing out at the paramedics and demand that they do more, that they bring his wife back, that the save her.

You have to save her! Why won't you save her? Please just save her!

Pathetic.

They ask who did this.

Ben Davies, he tells them.

By the time Harry leaves the house, they've determined I have never been there.

By the time Harry arrives at the station, they've determined that they were going to make the arrest.

And the coroners arrive. Swift, precise, uncaring. They take away numerous dead bodies every day, what's one more?

We all have roles to play.

Mine was to make Harry grateful for her. To make her grateful for him.

To show them that when they are pushed to their limits, then they will realise how much they need each other. That they will realise they need to stop taking each other for granted.

Except, they'll never do that now, will they?

And that was Harry's role.

And he played it perfectly. Executed to every detail. Performed with the Oscar-winning excellence of a professional.

As did I, my friends.

As did I.

WOULD YOU LIKE TWO BOOKS FOR FREE?

Join Rick's Reader's Group at www.rickwoodwriter.com/sign-up for updates and two free books...

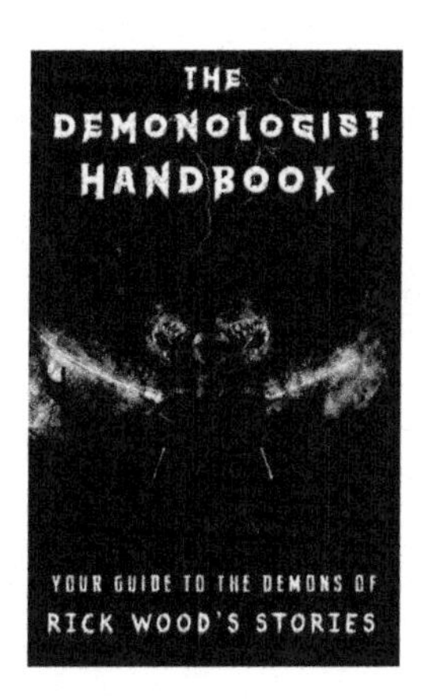

ALSO BY RICK WOOD

RICK
WOOD

TWELVE DAYS OF
CHRISTMAS HORROR

BLOOD SPLATTER BOOKS
18+
This Book Is
Full of BODIES
RICK WOOD

BLOOD SPLATTER BOOKS

18+

SHUTTER HOUSE

RICK WOOD

BOOK ONE IN THE SENSITIVES SERIES

THE SENSITIVES

RICK
WOOD

CIA
ROSE
BOOK
ONE

AFTER
THE DEVIL
HAS WON

Printed in Great Britain
by Amazon